Death On The Dial

A Brady Ellis RadioMurder

Jɪᴍ **BRADY**
Jɪᴍ **ELLIS**

Our Publishing Co.
Toledo, OH

Acknowledgements

To our good friends at Sidelines II, especially the bartenders, who put up with our constant arguing.

Thanks to Linda, and our other proofreaders for their diligence and comments. Any additional mistakes, we cheerfully claim as our own (blame Ellis... I always do).

This is a work of fiction. Any resemblance between the characters and persons living or dead is strictly in the warped imagination of the authors. The music, however, was very real.

Cover art by Cathy (Kit) Bernhoffer

ISBN 978-0-9830098-0-1

To Our Parents

Edward and Eloise,
James and Albirtha,
For blessings
far too numerous to count

Also by Jim Ellis

Double Blind
The Ghost of Boris Riley

ONE

Opening Declarations

"Do you have anything to declare?"

"Yeah, war," I joked, flashing my border pass, "the tanks are right behind me."

The border guard's mouth turned only slightly toward a grin. It was a joke I'd used on him before. Behind me, in Detroit, tensions were still pretty high after the riots during the summer of '67 and the assassination of Dr. King a little over a month ago. But over here in Windsor, Ontario, they continued to operate an outpost that reflected the atmosphere of "the World's Friendliest Border". They also knew tanks wouldn't fit through, and the last American invasion of Canada (even unofficially) was over 100 years back.

I was driving out of the South end of the tunnel from Detroit into Windsor, on my way home hoping to grab an hour or two of shut-eye before being back on the air for my 9 am radio show. The tunnel was finished in 1930, just in time for the last days of rum running, and became a link between cities that grew into the home of their respective auto industries. By 1968, the booze runners driving North into Detroit, turned into drug runners playing cat-and-mouse at the border with Customs Inspectors on both sides.

Although I worked, and now lived, on the Canadian side of the border, I still crossed back into the States at least a couple of times a week. From visiting Mom back in my hometown of Toledo, Ohio (about 50 road miles south), to concerts and events, most of them for my radio station, CKLW. I crossed for dates, dinners, and Tigers games. I like Detroit quite a bit, but these days I was happy to have the border behind me.

To save everybody's time at the border, workers that crossed frequently or commute get cards to show the inspectors. We knew all the rules for crossing and most of us are pretty careful. After a while, the guards begin to recognize you, and I think you get fewer vehicle inspections. In fact, I sometimes wonder how many people have bought real or counterfeit border passes in the hopes of making it easier to smuggle things across to Canada.

What did he expect me to declare? Should I declare it was pretty warm for the middle of May? That I was a bit drunk, a bit stoned and just a bit tweaked on mescaline? *Note to self: if I use mesc again… take the bridge home.* That I was only 21 years old and already had the coolest job in the world? That we were listening to trumpeter Hugh Masakela playing the hell out of "Grazing in the Grass"… and I could dig it… I could dig it, baby.

It had been a night of free beer, Motown music, dancing, singing, and what the folks out in California were calling free love, and I thought my life was perfect.

If I had any inkling about what was about to happen—how that night's fun would turn into murder and mayhem—I would have declared something. I might have declared I really didn't know anything about either of those girls, or that I had absolutely no idea what Armand and his friends, or even *my* friends, were up to.

I would have said I wasn't looking for trouble.

I would have said I didn't know how good things were.

I would have declared I didn't kill the girl.

I certainly would have declared *something!*

But I had no idea.

Two

A Few Free Beers

> One pill makes you larger, and one pill makes
> you small. And the ones that mother gives you
> don't do anything at all…
> —*White Rabbit,* Jefferson Airplane

It started Wednesday, May 15, 1968, just after 9 am at CLKW radio, where I had just started my nine to noon air shift.

A 50,000 watt clear channel—800 on the AM dial, the *Big 8* had recently become the top rated station in Detroit. Our mix of British Invasion, Motown, Soul, and straight up, old-fashioned American Rock 'n Roll had not only taken over Detroit, but had become the most popular stop for listeners in Toledo, Cleveland, and could be heard at night in 26 states and 4 provinces of Canada

Charlie Kelly, my buddy and the early morning man, stuck his head into the booth.

"Hey Brad, you got plans for tomorrow night?"

"Nothing particular. A few beers, probably."

"How about a few free beers?"

I grinned. "Sure… hang on."

Charlie stepped into the booth, closing the door as I opened my mic, the Johnny Mann singers sang, "Brad Walker, C—K—L—W", then the record rolled, "The Big 8, bathing your bod with boss vibrations, check out Booker T and the MGs, hitbound with Soul Limbo." I turned off the mic, and returned my attention to Charlie. "What's the deal?"

"Choker's playing at the Dearborn Stag House and Armand is buying," Charlie explained.

Choker Campbell's big band was a popular Detroit group. In spite of some local success, most of the band made their real income playing sessions for the more popular Motown artists.

The famed Motown sound was invented by people like Choker and enhanced by the famous singers and performers.

Armand Renault was a local record producer and promoter. Promoters were a pretty big deal in those days. With individual stations, and even the jocks making most of the decisions about which songs and which groups got the air time, promoters spent a good deal of time trying to get key people to hear their music. Although it was a few years after the big Payola scandal, when it was revealed that top DJ's were being paid cash to play some songs, there was still an opportunity for a promoter to influence decisions by wining and dining his radio people, and at least getting them to check out the songs for themselves.

On the other hand, radio folks found promoters useful as well. An extra source for what music was popular, particularly local sounds and groups. Promoters helped separate the wheat from the chaff, helping indentify which songs deserved consideration for airplay.

Armand probably wanted to impress a client or an investor and wanted us to show up wearing our "Big 8" jackets to show them that he had connections. It was OK with us. We got to hear good music, have fun, and never had to buy a drink. Not to mention enjoying the opportunity of being a minor celebrity and impressing the girls.

"Sure, Charlie," I said. "I'm in."

"Meet at my place?"

Charlie lived in Dearborn so it made sense to use his place as a base of operations for whatever the night would bring. That was one of the first things I learned when I got into the radio business—you never knew what the rest of the night would bring.

The *Dearborn Stag House* was a rent-by-night banquet hall/ballroom. You could hire it for any event. The main attraction was that they had a liquor license attached, so you could supply and serve drinks. It was a good place for a local band, just getting off the ground. You could rent out the hall, collect a buck or two at the door, and at the end of the day split the proceeds with the rest of your group. No promoters or managers needed.

Armand had hired a few big boys from the Michigan football team to keep an eye on the door. They waved us in, recognizing our Big 8 sport coats. We wore our coats because it was still the mark of being gentlemen in those days—besides, they were our ticket for the free drinks.

Our bright red jackets were pretty noticeable, or maybe he was looking for us, because Armand met us just inside the door and hustled us to a table near the bandstand. Charlie introduced him to Greg Ballard, our morning board operator, who he had not met. Armand then waved over a pretty black girl in a scarlet blouse and delightfully short black skirt.

"Look, kitten, these are my guys here. Make sure they get everything they need... and I do," he said with a wink, "mean everything. Oops, gotta go."

He quickly raced off to meet another group of six men all wearing suits, including a good-looking guy about my age, dressed head-to-toe in White.

"Investors," I said to Charlie.

"Hell, he's even getting money from the Ice Cream Man." He joked.

A bunch of kids were playing a Smokey Robinson tune and a handful of couples clung together on the dance floor. The crowd was a combination of Detroiters, local college kids, and a few from elsewhere. Unlike the city in those days, there seemed to be little racial tension or even that sort of casual segregation that often happens in mixed crowds. Everybody had come to enjoy the music and left the usual bullshit at the door.

The place continued to fill up and the kids, who I never got the name of, were replaced by Choker and his band and had gone from light and breezy Motown into some down home southern gut-bucket blues. A young fellow named Chambers had stunned me with an excellent rendition of Sam Cooke's "A Change is Gonna Come", and we were on our third beer or so when Charlie nudged me. I turned toward him and he casually opened his hand to reveal 3 capsules—one white and two black. They reminded me of the *Good 'n Plenty* candy I had tried when I was a kid (I didn't particularly like them).

"What is it," I asked

Charlie grinned, but shook his head. "That'd be telling," he drawled.

I hesitated. Charlie seemed to have a pill for every occasion but I generally passed on them. A couple of mornings when I was really drag-assing, I had agreed to have one of his "booster rockets" as a quick pick-up, but I was usually inclined to maintain a straight head. I mean, I know they never seemed to hurt Charlie, but... I nudged Greg on the other side of me. Still sipping his first beer, he shook his head then turned back to the bandstand. We generally let Ballard do the driving if he was going, because he rarely had more than a beer or two. That way, the rest of us always felt free to get tanked if we wanted—or in this case, got a little experimental...

Oh, what the hell, I finally decided.

"Does it matter which color?" I asked

He smiled slowly. "Nope."

I took the one black capsule while he took the other with his off-hand, gestured subtly with it, then joined me in taking it. Then dropped the third into his jacket pocket.

"Maybe for dessert," he said raising his brows Groucho-style.

I started laughing uncontrollably. And the pill hadn't taken effect, *yet.*

THREE

Wine, Women, & Song

Put on your hi-heel sneakers, 'cause we're
going out tonight…
—*Hi Heel Sneakers,* Tommy Tucker

My little pill kicked in while Sam George of the Capitols
was telling us a story about their appearance on *American
Bandstand.* I was sort of surprised to see Sam at one of
Armand's functions. A couple of years ago, they had asked
Armand to promote them and he turned them down. Of course,
they then turned around and had a top ten hit with "Cool Jerk",
followed by a national tour, Bandstand and all. Needless to say,
Armand tried not to remind himself of his decision by inviting
them to his events.

It began with little tingles in the arms and legs, then I began
to feel sort of warm and just vaguely dizzy. The room suddenly
seemed a bit brighter and more clearly focused, except for the
edges. The strangest thing was the time. Things seemed to have
either slowed down slightly, or sped up a bit. Enough to notice
but not enough to feel like it made a difference.

"Mescaline," Charlie reported after I began feeling the
effects. "Refined stuff, not that peyote shit some people get sick
on. First go?"

I must have nodded.

"Yeah, me too."

Really? My eyes widened. "Gift from a friend," he said as
if that explained everything.

It was hard to describe. Nothing had radically changed.
Beer usually relaxed me, but this mesc had me energized,
floating on air. I felt stronger, more confident, more aware. I
did notice that there was… seriously, a bit of a color trail to the
sounds I heard. Men's voices were sort of red; women's seemed
a little lighter-some sort of pink. The guitars were green, Horns
orange and the piano was a cool blue; nothing bright and glaring,

just barely perceivable and subtle. It struck me that they really were always there, I just had never noticed.

"You guys ought to do a number." Armand said.

"Sure." Charlie agreed quickly and casually, much to our surprise. Then he smiled at me. "But you know I'm not going up there alone."

"Oh, no…" I protested.

"Sure, it'll be fun, Brad. Didn't you say you were in a musical group back in school?"

"I was the DRUMMER!"

"You never did any singing?"

"Sure, in the school choir, but if we get up there singing some Four Freshmen harmony shit… they're going to kill us."

"Don't worry man, we'll be fantastic. We'll do Sam and Dave. You know their songs, right? You've seen the dance steps, just follow my lead."

OK, I had played the songs often enough, and I'd seen them and a couple of similar groups perform and I was sort of familiar with the dances they did, but it seemed a bit of a stretch to suggest that I was anywhere near knowing a full routine. But even while I was skeptical about pulling it off, the euphoria from my little pill was taking control.

The two of us hopped onto the bandstand, grinning broadly. "We're going to do our famous Sam and Dave medley," I proclaimed to Choker and the band. Even as they began to chuckle, I continued. "We'll do 'I Thank You', 'Hold On', then 'Soul Man.'"

Choker shook his head gently while still chuckling. "OK with us."

As we turned back toward the audience I said over my shoulder, "Stick to the original please, no vamping."

Once they stopped laughing, Charlie gave us an intro and we broke into the song and dance routine. The crowd began hooting and cheering and laughing. I was surprised how good we seemed to be. I had no idea Charlie could sing, but he was really quite good. We seemed to hit all the notes pretty well, we stayed in sync with the dance steps and put on a pretty good show.

By the time we shifted into "Soul Man", I was sweating like a whore in church and having a great time, but a stray thought crossed my mind. In the past few months, Charlie had been able to talk me into all kinds of outrageous stunts, both on and off the air, stuff that mostly turned out OK, always made me laugh, and a couple of times really worked for me. But, suddenly, I found myself wondering if Charlie was that persuasive, or was he just giving me a convenient excuse to do some of the things I was tempted to do anyway? We concluded the number by whipping off our jackets, twirling them overhead and flinging them off into the crowd. The applause washed over us, trailing waves of color. I looked back toward the band. Choker smiled and nodded, must have been pretty good... well... good enough anyway.

We made our way back through the crowd, people laughing and slapping us on the back.

"Hey, you guys were great," Armand enthused. "If you ever want to try your hand... I'll get a great deal for you on studio time."

Charlie and I grinned at each other, shaking our heads. We might have been entertaining, but we knew we'd never make it as musicians. That's how guys like me end up in the radio business. You love the music, but just don't have the sort of talent to be successful making it.

Charlie kept grinning at me.

"What?"

He still didn't say anything, just laughed. As we arrived at the table, we met two girls holding our jackets.

They were both about 5'6", one had dark hair in a short mod cut, piercing blue eyes, and beautiful bee-stung lips. The other was a bottle blonde with plenty of everything. I mean the dark haired girl had a nice trim figure, but her girlfriend had a shape that just wouldn't quit. She had pale brown eyes but there was something at the corner of her mouth that hinted that she was a woman who not only had bad thoughts, but might even enjoy them. Not always serious trouble, but certainly good for some mischief.

Charlie and I glanced at each other. Both would do, but how to decide?

"You guys are really talented." The blonde said.

"Well, thank you ma'am," Charlie was turning on the southern charm.

"I'm Jessie, and this is my friend, Linda."

"It's a pleasure." I said, introducing us.

"I listen to you guys all the time," Linda said, handing me my jacket. "You play great music."

"Thanks."

"I always wondered, how do you decide which songs to play... do you do that, or do they give you a list?"

I was a couple of sizes larger than Charlie, so there was little doubt whose jacket went to whom. Maybe the girls had already decided who got which. It was OK with me, I mean Jessie had the body, but I love a great pair of eyes.

"It's a bit of both," I answered. I spent a little time explaining formats and playlists and how we organized our shows.

After I finished the explanation, I reached for a chair and invited them to join us for a drink.

"I don't know," she said, with a gentle smile. "I think I'd rather dance. I mean, I'm not sure I can do any of those fancy steps you guys did..."

"Oh, don't worry," I answered, "I think we can get things slowed down a little... rumor is we know the band."

Almost on cue, the band switched to a slow blues tune. When we got onto the dance floor, I was a bit surprised to find she snuggled right up to me like we knew each other better than we did. On the other hand, this sort of dancing certainly encouraged getting to know each other better.

As the next song began, I looked to my right and saw Charlie and Jessie in a pretty good clinch on the floor as well. We seemed to be making pretty good progress.

After a bit of dancing, we sat and had a few drinks. We stayed with beer, the girls had rum and Cokes. After a bit of drinking and conversation, Jessie piped up.

"So you guys are Canadian?"

"No, ma'am," Charlie said. "I'm from Tupelo Mississippi... just like Elvis." Actually, Charlie was from Memphis, but it was close enough.

"I'm from Toledo."

"Toledo, Ohio... really?" *How many other Toledos are there around here?*

"Yeah, but I'm living over in Windsor."

"You know, I've never been to Canada." Linda said.

"Me, neither," Jessie said. "How tough is it to go over?"

"Oh, it's easy as pie," Charlie said. You'll have to come over some time and see the place."

"Now you live over there, too, Charles?"

"No, I live right here in Dearborn."

"Good. Then, we'll go to your place." Jessie said. "Lin and I have got another little dance routine I think you boys are *really* going to enjoy."

FOUR
Chucklehead

Bottle of wine, fruit of the vine, when you
gonna let me get sober…
        -Bottle of Wine,
        Jimmy Gilmer and the Fireballs

"Must have been one hell of a night."

Mac McCarthy was not only the ace morning newshound for CKLW's 20/20 news, but for the last several weeks was my roommate. We were sharing an apartment at the Holiday Inn. Long story. Tell you later.

He was off to work by the time I made it home, so he had come downstairs from the news studio into our lounge, or bullpen, to catch up a bit.

"It was pretty good," I answered. "How did your evening go?"

Mac had one of those classic bass voices that all of us were at least a little jealous of. He drew more fan mail than most of us and for some reason, the French Canadian girls in particular used to break out in the cold sweats just listening to him. One of the girls at the station had set Mac up with a girlfriend, which he saw as a surer thing than our concert.

"Very nice. I think Jeanne Marie had a good time. It was a bit difficult at first. Her English was a little shaky."

"But, of course, her French was excellent," I said with a subtle grin.

He grinned back. "You're a sick man, Walker."

"No news there."

"I figured you must have done OK yourself, seeing as you didn't even make it home."

"Well, you know how it is, Mac, you can sleep when you're dead… or married."

We were both chuckling when the door flew open, and our Program Director, Fred Wilson, marched in, his face flushed.

"What the hell were you thinking, Walker?" He ranted. "I heard about your little stunt last night! Now, I might expect this sort of foolishness from a troublemaker like Kelly, but..."

He stopped in mid sentence; Mac's presence suddenly registered with him.

"What the hell are you doing here, McCarthy? The news department is upstairs."

"Just saying good morning to my friend before he goes on the air," He said, very coolly.

"You'd be surprised how many people," I said with sarcastic authority, "fail to observe civilized courtesies, like greeting... or knocking..."

"Alright, alright," Fred said dismissively, "Piss off, McCarthy."

"Of course," Mac said, inclining his head gently, "but before I take my leave, I'd like to wish you both a very pleasant good morning."

As he got to the door, he offered a parting shot.

"See ya... Chuckles."

"What?" he spun back, but only saw the door swinging closed.

Fred was a record promotion type who didn't seem to know anything useful about radio programming... nor did he seem to have any clues about production. We were even less impressed with his use of authority or his ability to work with others. How the hell he got the job was a mystery to us all, although I always suspected he had a picture of our general manager, Bob Bluster, in a pink tutu.

Fortunately, we all developed a policy of ignoring "Chucklehead Fred", and either did things the way they had been done, or the way we thought best, while always pretending to pay attention to his ranting and screamed orders.

A few of us had taken to calling him Chuckles, sometimes to his face when he became particularly insufferable. He was annoyed by the nickname, but seemed to have no idea what it meant. I did hear him ask our star evening DJ if people thought he had a bad sense of humor. Perhaps a question that answered itself.

"OK, what seems to be the problem, Fred?"

"Do I need to remind you two clowns that when you wear those blazers, you are representing CKLW and need to act professionally."

"What the hell are you babbling about?"

"I'm talking about that little stunt you pulled last night. I've got my phone ringing off the hook over your little unauthorized appearance."

"Unauthorized... look, it was a local music event. We wore the jackets because it was good publicity for the station. We want people to know that we're always where the good music is, not just voices on the radio."

"Then you got up on stage and made asses of yourselves! I heard from several people this morning... they're laughing at us."

"If people are laughing, they're probably laughing at those two crazy *guys* from CKLW, not the whole station. Besides, they might be laughing because they had a good time."

Fred continued to glare. I tried to keep a straight face.

"Listen, Fred, I'm sorry if *your* friends didn't enjoy our little number, but most of the folks there, seemed to love it. I'll bet that for every person who called you to complain, there were several who thought it was good fun and might even take time out to listen to a couple of guys who can have a good time and are willing to put their dignity on the line to entertain people."

"Listen, Walker..."

He never finished the rant because the intercom rang.

"Brad Walker, line three." The voice said.

"Brad Walker," I said.

"Hello, Brad Walker," a sultry voice answered. "This is Jessie Royce. We met last night."

"How could I forget?"

"I called to let you know that my friend Linda and I really enjoyed the show you boys put on last night."

Well," I said, winking at Fred, "I'm very glad to hear you enjoyed the show."

Fred paced the room impatiently as Jessie continued. "Actually, we were hoping you guys might be up..." I smiled as she paused, "to a repeat performance of that little dance the four of us did, maybe this afternoon? Linda and I are Kelly girls and we should get off early today."

I leaned back in my chair. "Well, I can't actually speak for Charlie, but I'm pretty certain something can be arranged."

"Super. You talk to Charles, and I'll call a bit later with details. In the meantime, let me give you my number... 555-5789."

"...5-7-8-9... hey just like in the Wilson Pickett song."

"Talk to you soon, handsome."

"Bye."

I hung up and swung back to face Fred.

"A satisfied customer from last night," I mused with a huge grin. "What was it you wanted to talk about again, Fred? I've got to be on the air in a minute or two."

He fumed for a minute.

"Oh, never mind."

He left the room muttering to himself.

FIVE
Twisting by the Pool

...gotta keep movin', never gonna slow down,
you can have your funky world, see ya 'round.
        —*Ramblin' Gamblin' Man,* Bob Seger

Jessie's call had me a bit distracted. I had assumed that the two girls had sort of chosen their playmate last night, but perhaps the possibilities were still open. Was she making a play for me, or just being the social secretary?

Allan Douglas, my board operator, yelled into the intercom, "Wake up, Walker... the Temps need a follow up here." He was getting just a little testy.

I shook my head. "Sorry man, I'm a little off this morning. Give me the 'more music' fast to fast... then #21, the new Aretha tune."

Almost instantly, the jingle hit the air followed by the piano riff leading into Aretha's latest hit, "Think". I hit my mic and roared: "10:09 at C-K-L-W with Brad Walker and soul sister #1 AREETHAAAA!!!" As the vocal immediately came up on the song, Allan raised his arms like a football referee. "There you go, way to hit it!" he said. "Now, what the hell is with you today, man?"

"Oh, man," I answered, "you wouldn't believe what happened last night"

Allan laughed. "Greg told me about you and Charlie... he said you were great!"

I smiled and said. "Did he tell you about the two young lovelies that brought us our jackets after we flung them into the audience?"

"He told me that they took you home or something".

I smiled and said: "Yeah, it's the 'or something' that has my mind wandering."

Allan studied me with amusement. We were usually engaged in full conversation during the show, as we discussed the weighty matters of life, but today I was distracted, quiet, and slightly hung-over.

The previous night had been a lot of new experiences for me... the mescaline, the on stage performance with Charlie, and the wild night with the four of us in Charlie's king size bed. I don't know if it was new ground for Charlie, who was about seven years older than I, but I had certainly never done a mix and match like that, not to mention a couple of those double combinations. All he said when I stepped into the studio to relieve him at three minutes before nine was: "Bradley, we just found us a goldmine!"

I nodded. Calling me Bradley was an inside joke between us, as my name isn't really Bradley.

"What's even better is that I got a phone number." He taunted, grinning wolfishly.

"Well, I just did you one better. I talked to Jessie... the blonde, and she not only gave me her number, but the girls already want a repeat performance today!"

"Do we have to sing first?" he chuckled,

"No," I said. "And I suspect most of the dancing is going to be horizontal, again."

"Hey, sounds good," said Charlie. "Think I'm gonna hit the sack at your place for a couple hours".

"Sure, See you later," I nodded.

Charlie occasionally caught a nap there when the two of us were doing something together in the afternoon. Mac and I let a few of our co-workers use our place on occasion. It was close to the station and, as a hotel, it had daily maid service... the perfect bachelor pad! In fact, one of our more popular jocks used it several times a month, and always left the maid a very healthy tip. Our sources in the hotel kept us informed of the extra-curricular activities.

As the morning went on, I told Allan some of the details of the previous evening. I mentioned that I really liked both girls, but didn't know which to pursue. Was there any future, or was it just a one hit wonder?

Allan shook his head and said, "Man, I sometimes wonder why I got married at nineteen and have to miss all this stuff".

I thought about his lovely wife, and how she would bring
lunch when we worked weekends or stop by with pizza and said,
"Nah, Corrina is the best! You're lucky to have her!"

He smiled and said, "You are absolutely right! She loves me,
has a great job and doesn't bitch when I go out for a beer with
you guys."

I got back to the apartment at 12:10 and roused Charlie from
the living room couch with a cold bottle of Labatt's Blue pressed
against his forehead. He jumped up, swore violently, then
laughed and took a swig of the golden nectar.

Jessie, true to her word, had indeed called me during my
show, and said the girls were off the entire afternoon, and gave
me an address in fashionable Grosse Point Farms. We headed
out at about 2:30. I followed Charlie to his place in Dearborn.
He parked his '66 Caddy in the parking garage, ran inside to get
a joint, then jumped into my Cutlass convertible as we headed
out east on I-94 toward Grosse Pointe Farms. I knew the way
pretty well, since my friend Casey and I had lived together in
next-door Grosse Pointe Woods for the better part of the past
year. It was unseasonably warm for mid-May, a perfect
convertible day, and we were listening to our colleague Big Bill
Davis playing Bob Seger's "Ramblin' Gamblin' Man" on the
Big 8, as Charlie lit up his joint. He, as usual, offered me a hit,
and I, as always, OK, almost always, declined. I never did care
for the way it made me feel, especially when driving… it just
seemed to take forever to get anywhere. I mostly just drank
beer. Charlie enjoyed a few hits, flicked the hot ash into the
ashtray, then put the remainder of the joint in his cigarette pack
and lit up a Winston. He offered me one, and I took it. I might
as well, since he had swiped the pack from my carton back at the
apartment. Charlie bought Marlboros when necessary, but
preferred to smoke o.p.'s, especially mine!

Traffic was light, we made good time, and were soon
seeking the Beacon Hill Rd. address Jessie had given me.

Charlie and I whistled as we pulled up to a huge colonial
style mansion, and thought, "Wow!"

He grinned, "I think we hit the jackpot, kid, these chicks are
not only sexy, but *rich*." We later learned that Linda's father had
made a small fortune in the construction business.

Charlie and I left the Cutlass sitting on the long brick driveway at the side of the house behind the open one of the four garage doors behind a red Pontiac GTO convertible.

"Must be Linda's," I remarked. Charlie was still staring wide-eyed at the huge house, almost drooling.

We grinned at each other as I joked, "I don't think we're in Memphis anymore, Toto!"

Linda stepped around the far side of the garage. She had mentioned she was living in what the real estate agents call an "in-law suite", an apartment with a separate entrance from the main house. It was an ideal arrangement for protective parents to let 21-year old Linda have her privacy, but still live safe at home.

"Hey, guys!" Our lovely Linda was wearing a blue bikini, which almost, but not quite, matched her eyes. "You timed it perfectly... We just got here ourselves."

Charlie looked at her and drawled, "We pride ourselves on good timing, babe."

Linda looked at me with a smirk, and said: "I know. I remember the demonstration you guys did last night."

I think I blushed a bit, knowing she wasn't talking about our stage performance.

"Come on out back. It's such a warm day, I figured we should hang out by the pool."

The back "yard" was about an acre of beautifully designed landscaping. The entire place looked like it required a staff of several people to keep it in shape, but today no one was in sight. It appeared that the four of us had the place to ourselves, which, I thought, could make for an interesting next few hours. I was right.

Linda, who seemed to be reading my mind, said: "Nobody's home, my folks are at a convention in Las Vegas, and my sister is spending the night with her best friend, so we have the place all to ourselves."

Charlie looked at the pool a bit nervously. He had a brand new hairpiece to disguise his rapidly receding hairline, and I figured he was worried about submerging it in water. But that was his problem.

Jessie made her entrance about then, wearing what, on most women, would be called a modest one piece chartreuse swimsuit. Charlie whistled.

"Thank you, Charles," Jessie purred, as she posed. She knew she looked fabulous, hell she could wear a trash bag and make it look good.

"Bar's open" called Linda, as my attention turned to the beauty in the blue bikini on the incredibly appointed patio, "Who's thirsty?"

"What a palace," I said, as I pulled up a stool at the bar, "can I have a beer?"

"Sure", said Linda, "Daddy has Stroh's on tap, or would you like something else in a can?"

"I'll take the Stroh's, thanks."

"Me too," said Jessie from behind me.

"Me three," chimed in Charlie.

As we all sat and enjoyed a cold beer on a warm afternoon, the Big 8 provided the background music. "Motormouth" Mike Waters was having a great time, occasionally pushing the bounds of good taste in a very funny way. Mike came out of Shirley Ellis' rhyming song "The Name Game" by saying: "C'mon, Let's do CHUCK."

We all laughed. "How does he get away with that?" Linda asked.

"He won't," Charlie, not a real fan of Mike's style, grumbled. "One of these days, Chucklehead Fred is just gonna kick his ass out."

Fred had warned Mike many times to keep it clean, but Mike refused to tone it down.

Later we would learn that the "CHUCK" bit was that final straw for Chucklehead, and Mike was canned. Luckily, he was hired immediately by our previous program director Drew Yarborough, who was now in Philly, and had a better sense of humor. We all missed Drew a lot!

But I digress.

After a second round of drinks, Jessie suggested that we should hit the pool. Just for form's sake, I mentioned that neither Charlie nor I had brought swim suits. Jessie laughed.

"Who need's 'em?" She said, deftly removing hers and jumping into the sparkling pool. Linda dove in behind her, leaving the bikini on the deck as well.

"C'mon in, the water's fine," she yelled.

Charlie and I probably set a new land speed record getting undressed, and into the pool!

We had a great time swimming and splashing, Charlie doing his best to keep his head above water. After a little mutual horse play, Linda and I paired up, as did Jessie and Charlie. We were tangled together about waist deep on the steps at the shallow end, and things were progressing nicely, when a voice came from behind me on the Patio: "Hey Lin... oh, great! A pool party. Can we join you?"

I looked over my shoulder and saw four teenagers, including a girl who could only have been Linda's sister, with big grins on their faces, getting undressed.

SIX

A Brush With Fame

I could feel Linda's body stiffen in my arms.

"Brandy, what the hell are you doing here?" she exclaimed.

Linda was flabbergasted. It didn't take a lot of insight to realize she was really pissed off with her younger sister and her friends for barging in to interrupt our own afternoon festivities.

The kids had shed their clothes and jumped into the pool at the deep end, but Charlie and Jessie were still entwined and oblivious for the moment.

Little sister swam over to us.

"Hey, Lin," she teased. "Who's your friend?"

"My sister, Brandy," she said, through almost clenched teeth. "Brad Walker."

"The radio guy? Ooh, Mr. Big 8. Hi there."

She offered a hand, which I shook awkwardly, then she splashed off to join her friends.

As Charlie and Jessie became aware of their company, they began to laugh and splash with the kids. Meanwhile, Linda looked at me and said, "Let's go inside. I'll give you a tour of the place, then we can find a quiet place to get back to what we were doing... I know this might be hard to believe, but I prefer privacy, really!"

It did seem a bit contradictory, considering we hadn't exactly had any private encounters, but I nodded. "Me too."

We left our clothes on the patio, and moved quietly into the massive house. As we walked along she asked questions about living in Windsor and the radio station. We were walking through the kitchen, heading toward the door of her suite, which was probably bigger than the apartment Mac and I shared.

"So even though you *play* James Brown, they wouldn't let you interview him?"

"Nope. Our Programming Director, Fred, said, 'This is a music station, not news...' Chucklehead."

"OK. Who was the most famous person you ever had come to the station?"

"Dr Martin Luther King, I guess."

"Seriously? When was that?"

"Back in March, just a few weeks before he was killed. It started as an ordinary day, playing the tunes and taking requests on the hitline, when I looked up and saw Fred, our moron program director, standing outside the studio door. Well, he usually had better sense than to hang around there, knowing how territorial we were.

Then I saw the three black gentlemen, with him. It didn't make sense at first until I recognized Dr. King! Fred slithered into the studio and explained that he had come by to be interviewed at our sister TV station, Channel 9, and wanted to know if he could visit the famous 'Big 8!' I looked past Fred and signaled for them to come on in. Just as they walked in, Allan shouted 'Coming up!' I held my hand up like a traffic cop, and grabbed my earphones with the other. I turned up the speaker in the studio just as the jingle came on... 'More music...C K L W', I hit the mic button and said 'it's 10:27 at CKLW with Brad Walker, and the latest from soul brother #1, James Brown... Whooo... "I Got the Feelin'!"' I took off the earphones, and Dr. King was grinning from ear to ear.

"'My man!' Dr. King said, 'You guys play the *best* music!' I stood up and walked over to him and shook his hand. I said, 'Brad Walker, sir, a pleasure to meet you.' He clasped my hand with both of his, and said, 'The pleasure is mine, brother!' He introduced me to his companions, and said, 'At last I get to see where it all happens, this station is the greatest!' I, of course, agreed with him and thanked him for dropping in. They left the studio, and I sat down, stunned. I had met one of America's true heroes.

"It freaked me out about a month later when he was assassinated. I mean it seemed really unfair to all of us... the man had done so much good, and still had so much left to do."

"So, what was he like?"

"Very personable. He treated you like you were the only person in the room. He was also a bit bigger than I thought. He seemed like was intelligent and caring and obviously pretty fearless. But he also seemed exhausted. He looked a lot older than he was."

"And he had actually heard of you?"

"He was certainly familiar with the station. Our signal covers a monstrous portion of North America, especially at night when AM radio signals travel farther…"

"So what did he really think?"

"I think he was like most of our visitors. They hear all this music and the big sound, and they find this sort of simple little place, and I think they feel like they're missing something. They feel like there has to be more to it, you know?"

She nodded. I was looking around her apartment as she led me by the hand toward her bedroom.

"Wow", I said, "This is beautiful!"

"I love it", Linda agreed, "it's the perfect way to be on my own, without having my parents worry, like they did when I went away to school."

"Don't tell me... University of Michigan?

"Yeah, I went for about a year and a half, but I had to come back home."

"Had to?"

"Oh, you know what I mean. Anyway, I have the place to myself."

"Sure, but what happens when your sister grows up?" I said.

"By that time we figure I will be married and gone, and Brandy can have this place to herself."

An ironic twist on the corner of her smile said it all. The hunt was on, and I was a potential target. I kind of liked the idea.

About half an hour later, we were lying in a beautiful canopy bed, totally spent. "This is a first," I said, "I've never been in bed with a roof before."

Linda looked into my eyes and said, "It is a beautiful bed, isn't it? My mom and I won it on the TV quiz show *Strike it Rich*. I was 8 years old, and we went all the way to New York City. They took us through the studio and showed us how everything worked and there were so many people and they treated me just like I was a fairy princess or something. Then they put us on the stage with all of those people watching and the bright lights and they asked me what I wanted more than anything in the world. And I wished for a big canopy bed, and somebody called the 'Heartline' just for me and made my dream come true."

Just then, there was a loud knocking at the door. "Hey guys, open up!" Jessie called, "We want to play too."

SEVEN
Studio Session

> I got a thing, you got a thing, everybody's
> got a thing...
> >   —*Everybody's Got a Thing*, Funkadelic

It was Saturday morning and I was driving across the Ambassador Bridge with the top down. It would have been faster to go through the tunnel to get to Woodward Avenue, but it was a beautiful spring day and I wanted to enjoy the drive. The wind in my face would give me a chance to clear my head after that pool party. I was on my way to Armand's studio, WestGrand, a small, nondescript cinder block building just off Detroit's main drag.

I had been on the air near the end of my shift yesterday:

> *It's 11:48 at CKLW, Brad Walker movin' you up toward the noon hour and your friend and mine, Big Bill Davis, with another Friday afternoon of the music that motivates the Motor City. Here's Sam Cooke... 'A Change is Gonna Come.' (Music)*

As I finished, the request line flashed.

"CKLW, what can we play for you?"

"Brad, my friend..."

"Hey Armand, what's shaking?"

"First, I wanted to call you and thank you for coming out to last night's concert. I hope you fellows enjoyed the music... and the dancing?"

"Yeah, it was a good time, thanks for inviting us."

"You do know I was very serious about giving you fellows a chance to try your hand as singers—you, of course, remember the Big Bopper..."

"Started out as a DJ... OK, enough soft soap, what can I do for you?"

"I was hoping you fellows didn't have any plans for lunch tomorrow."

"Don't think so."

"Then you can maybe do me a favor. Do you remember the Parliaments?"

"The Parliaments…"

The Parliaments were what some people called a one hit wonder. They had a hit with the song "I Want to Testify," and an album that was, at best, a mild success.

"Well, they're changing the entire group. The lead singer and the rhythm section are working on a brand new sound. Something really radical."

"Radical?"

"Trust me, my friend; this is going to revolutionize the music business… something you have never heard before."

Nothing new in this pitch. All promoters and producers hype their groups as playing something revolutionary. Even at the age of 21, if I had a nickel for every 'new' sound…

"I know, I *know*… it sounds like the usual A&R hype, but what I am hoping is that you will come to hear for yourself. I know I am very excited, but I have been listening from the beginning. I need a pair of, well, clean ears to react to the music."

It wasn't like I had plans or anything, I had vaguely considered crossing back to the States to see my friend Casey, but we had made no concrete plans. It might be interesting, and Armand usually bought a good lunch.

"OK. I guess I can give it a listen."

"Excellent. Come by about 11. We can hear the group, then have lunch. There are a few other groups I want to talk to you about."

Damn. I knew there was going to be a hitch. He was going to pitch us his whole catalog.

When I arrived, the studio was full—over a dozen musicians, two drum kits, bass and guitars, trumpet and trombones, sax, pianos and various other instruments were squeezed into the studio. I walked into the control room while the entire group was playing together.

There were two engineers, Charlie, Armand, and his partner Bennie Morris. I always thought of Bennie as the silent partner

because he said almost nothing and as far as I could tell, never
did anything. At well over 300 pounds, he almost made his 5
foot 9 inch frame look square. I had wondered if part of his role
was as a bodyguard. In 1968's Detroit, a character like Armand
spent a lot of time running around black neighborhoods in a city
rife with racial tension. It would make sense to have a man-
mountain like Bennie available to back you up.

Armand turned to me excitedly.

"See, do you not think this is an exciting sound?"

I listened for a few seconds. The large group did produce an
unusual depth of sound and the size of the rhythm section gave
them an infectious beat. But I also thought it was still a bit raw.
It was going to take some time to get all of those guys on the
same musical page.

I nodded a little. "Yeah, I think it's interesting." Charlie
nodded in agreement.

"Good. I am glad you like it. I felt we needed someone who
knew what the modern listener might like. The rest of us are
maybe a bit too close? You must meet George."

"Hey, what's happenin' baby." George Clinton greeted us as
he came out of the studio.

"Brad Walker." I introduced myself, and then Charlie.

"C K L W... The Big 8. Y'all play great music. I knew
you'd dig this sound, I mean you got the whole *funkadelic* thing
going on yourself."

"Funkadelic?" I asked.

The others grinned at me.

"Yeah, see the way I get it, the white boys over there," he
pointed vaguely toward what might be California, "are doing a
really cool Psychedelic sort of thing that we really dig, while the
brothers here," pointing down, "are straight up funking. What
y'all do is play it all-the funk and the 'delic, and what we want to
do is play the funk and 'delic together."

"Everything's funkadelic these days with George," Armand
said. "We all have the fever."

I nodded. "I like your sound."

"We got a lot of work left, baby, but we'll get there. So
what about you? How'd a kid from Canada learn so much about
funk music."

"Well, I'm not from Canada, I just work over there. I'm
actually from Toledo."

"Toledo! I know Toledo… I'm from Toledo. Where you from?"

"West Toledo… Sylvania Avenue, Willys Parkway."

"Yeah, I know that area. My cousin works at the Jeep plant over there. Where'd you go to school."

"DeVilbiss."

He shook his head.

"I can't get over it… Toledo!"

We grinned at each other for a moment. Then he stirred.

"OK, he said, let's do that thang"

He stepped back into the studio.

"That Thang?" I said with a raised eyebrow.

They played a tune called *Everybody's Got a Thing.* Whatever they were, they surely weren't the old Parliaments.

"Hey," I said to George when he returned to the control room, "that's a good song."

He smiled. "Yeah, I like it, but there's something still not right about the drums or something maybe in the intro…"

I thought for a moment.

"Maybe if they just used the bass, with the high hats," I muttered to Charlie.

"What was that?" George turned to me. I hadn't realized I was that loud.

"I don't know, I was just thinking… on the intro, if you could get the drummer to use the high hats, and bass... look, it would probably be easier to just show you."

He looked me up and down.

"You *play* drums?" he asked, a bit surprised.

"Since I was a kid."

"You any good?"

"I guess I'm OK," I shrugged, sounding cockier than I felt. "I think I can at least give you an idea of what I'm talking about."

"Hey, y'all," George joked, "we got us a white boy with rhythm."

The musicians all laughed and even Bennie began rumbling a chuckle. I didn't exactly laugh out loud, but it was pretty funny, even to me.

"OK, Toledo, let's see what you got."

I had become bit nervous with the other musicians, but I managed to calm down by reminding myself that I was just fooling around and I couldn't really screw up unless I broke something.

"You see, instead of doing this…" I demonstrated the way the drummer had played it. "…roll the tape and I'll show you."

The engineer rolled the song, minus the drum track, and I played my variation, replacing his single tap on the snare with a steady rhythm on the high hat cymbals, along with a few bass drum off beats, then, during the instrumental bridges, swung into a wild riff, reminiscent of "Wipe Out" which surprised even me. When I finished, the drummer nodded and the other musicians murmured assent. A few even clapped a couple of times.

"Hey man," said George from the control room. "That was great. Just the funkadelic we were looking for."

"Thanks," I answered into the overhead mic. "Anyway, you might want to do it like that."

"*Do* it like that? Man, we just *did it* like that. Wasn't you here for that?"

I was stunned. "You mean… that was a take?!"

George chuckled. "It sure is now, 'cause we took it, brother. You don't have a problem with that, do you?"

I could feel the big cheese-eating grin crossing my face.

"No! Of course not, if you think it works… that's cool."

EIGHT
Crossing Over

It's my party and I'll cry if I want to…
—*It's My Party*, Leslie Gore

"He's throwing his own party?" Linda asked, incredulously.

It was early Friday afternoon and the girls had knocked off early. Chucklehead Fred was throwing a party for his birthday, but most of the station employees were working until five. Charlie and I were, of course, already done for the week. Mac was over in Detroit at City Hall, and we were just killing time.

"Well, he is sort of new at the station…" I pointed out. "And to be honest, most of us don't like him very much."

"So why are we going?"

"Well," Charlie said with that grin, "he is buying the beer…"

"It *is* Friday…" I continued.

"Besides we know he's an asshole at work, but that doesn't mean he might not be a fun guy to go drinking with."

Jessie nodded. "And as you know, Lin, sometimes it's a good idea to go along with co-workers in order to keep peace at work."

"Some of the girls are even probably going 'cause they've never been in Sid's Bridge House," I said.

"OK, what's so special about Sid's Bridge House?" Jessie asked.

Charlie and I looked at each other.

"Women aren't usually allowed." I said.

Linda's eyes narrowed. "What do you mean, women aren't allowed?"

"No women allowed in the bar."

"You mean, something old fashioned, like, no unescorted women sitting at the bar?"

"No, I mean it's some Canadian law. Women are not allowed in taverns."

"You've got to be shitting me!" Jessie said.

"Nope. The state… province of Ontario still keeps taverns men only."

"But it's 1968," Linda squeaked. "Surely…"

"They haven't changed the law, yet. Don't yell at me, you might have noticed that I actually *like* women."

Linda smoldered. "So you're telling me women can't drink in Canada?"

I tried to adopt a soothing tone. "No, they can drink all they want… just not in taverns."

"Sure," Charlie explained, "they can drink in restaurants."

"What's the difference between restaurants and taverns?" Linda demanded.

I couldn't resist. "Restaurants serve food," I deadpanned.

The girls glared at me.

"They also close earlier than the bars… 11 o'clock. Taverns can stay open until midnight, but there are two unusual rules. The first is that all bars have to be, technically, hotels."

"Meaning you can get a room at Sid's?" Jessie asked.

"Yeah, but I bet you really wouldn't want it—at least not until after you've had your shots. The second rule is no women."

"But that's just stupid!" Linda exclaimed.

"The law might be stupid, but they have liquor agents that are paid to enforce it and they would shut the place down."

"Why don't the women here object?"

"Don't know that they don't. There is one sort of advantage for the women… If your guy is going out to the tavern with the boys, you don't have to worry about him picking up a girl."

"Unless she works there." Jessie said.

"None working at Sid's. Don't know if that's the law or not."

"We shouldn't go," Linda said, emphatically. "It's injustice and we shouldn't stand for it."

"Oh c'mon, Lin, aren't you curious? Besides we can always make a 'wrong turn' and completely shock all the old fuddy-duddies at the bar."

"Or start a riot," Charlie offered.

Oh, great Charlie… encourage them.

"Then again Lin, the guys wouldn't have anything to gain by embarrassing their co-workers, and they really should make an appearance."

She stood up and stretched languorously, then reached for the zipper of her dress.

"Besides, we've got a couple of hours to kill," she said as her dress fluttered to the floor. "Maybe the boys will have us too worn out to protest."

For all his other faults, Chucklehead was actually a pretty cordial host. He was significantly more friendly than he ever seemed to be at work; he told decent stories and kept the drinks coming.

Many of the guys came stag, but a couple brought their wives, much to the chagrin of the office girls, some of whom were carrying on with the married guys. Somewhere between Detroit City Hall, where he did interviews in the afternoon, and the bar, Mac had managed to collect an outstanding tall redhead named Nancy.

The couple of dozen who had been there at the beginning of the festivities had dwindled to about ten and we decided to call it a night. By the time we actually got out of there, a few people invited for a capper had become the entire party moving to room 404 of the Holiday Inn.

The Windsor Holiday Inn had four 'chalet-style' apartments on their top floor. Mac and I had been living there since April. The whole thing actually started when Dr. King was shot. The CK management, worried that all of their US-based announcers would be caught on the wrong side of the border by riots and unrest, brought all of us across to Windsor and put us up at the Holiday Inn, just across Riverside Drive from the station.

During that next week we found out that the Hotel had the bi-level apartments on the top floor. They were not only perfectly located, but very reasonably priced. This was a perfect bachelor's pad. Short walk to work, maid service, room service, a front desk to take phone messages (long before cell phones or answering machines) and The Beer Store delivered! Mac and I thought we had died and gone to heaven.

We got everybody into the apartment and supplied drinks. We even found some chips and snacks for our guests. I had gone upstairs for a moment and was heading back down when I heard a familiar laugh coming from the kitchen. I moved over toward Linda.

"I thought Jessie was going home with Charlie?" I said.

"I did too, but she just came in here a minute ago with what's-his-name… your boss."

My jaw dropped. "She brought *Chucklehead?*"

"I guess so; I saw them together when they got here."

After a couple of rounds, a few had peeled off and Jessie came strolling out of the kitchen arm in arm with Bennett Cole, one of our board operators.

She planted herself on my lap and nibbled at my ear.

"Bradley, I just love this place," she murmured.

She took a look around the room at the guests, many of them just sitting and relaxing, listening to the music.

"This place is sort of dead," she complained. "What you need is something to crank up the voltage. Hey, Lin," she leaned toward her vaguely, "want to go halves on a kilo of coke?"

It was a loud enough whisper to stop a couple of nearby conversations. Linda, who usually seemed to go along, looked genuinely shocked.

"I've got a source… We can make money and party, too!"

Linda shook her head. "You're crazy…"

"Oh, come on, it isn't like you never used it before…"

"But Jess, drug dealing involves very dangerous people. Not to mention the police. I bet the Canadian government would really come down on you for bringing Coke across the border."

"Fine," she pouted, "be a pussy."

Linda shook her head at me while Jessie fluttered off again.

"She's always proposing all kinds of outrageous shit," she said. "You just learn to ignore most of it. I've got to tell you, sometimes she seems just plain dangerous."

I nodded. They sometimes sort of reminded me of Charlie and I, how he always seemed to be the one behind the outrageous ideas and I always seemed to go along.

It was about a half an hour later, a lull in the music and a pause in the conversation prompted Mac to notice something.

"Do you hear water running?" he asked.

There was really no question that the shower was running. We looked at each other, quizzically.

Linda leaned over toward me. "Jessie," she said in a half-whisper.

I looked around the room. "She's in there with Chucklehead?"

"He's the best bet," she said, "but you know Jessie."

We kept talking and drinking. Conspiratorial laughter punctuating the moment every time the silence disclosed that the water was still running.

"I can't believe somebody's using your shower," Nancy said, giggling. "I mean it really seems kind of rude."

"Well, I guess some people are really desperate to get clean," I said with a half smile.

Mac shook his head. "Nobody takes that long to get clean."

"That's a lot more about getting dirty." Linda said.

After a few minutes I headed upstairs. "I'm going to have to go," I grumbled, to no one in particular. "And hey, it is my bathroom."

I knocked as I walked in. "Don't mind me. I'm just taking care of a little business of my own. You just keep doing whatever you're doing."

I heard a male grunt and female giggle in response.

By the time I got back downstairs, the party was breaking up. Mac had left to take Nancy home and the others were starting to head out as well.

Linda and I were the only ones left when Fred dashed down the steps from upstairs.

"Thanks for having me," he stammered. "This is a nice place." Then he hit the door like someone was after him.

Jessie sauntered down the steps wearing my bathrobe. She smiled at me predatorily.

"You know how it is, Bradley," she purred. "Sometimes a girl just has to come clean."

I shook my head. "But Fred?"

"Well, I felt sorry for him. He had to throw his own birthday party, and there wasn't even any cake."

"So you decided to blow out his candle for him?" Linda joked.

"Well… what he lacked in talent, he made up for in enthusiasm."

"Why would I want to know this?" I muttered.

She stretched out on the coffee table.

"So, Brad, where's your roommate?"

"Took his date home."

She crossed her arms, rubbing her sides.

"Too bad," she purred, "I was hoping we could get to know each other better. Maybe at breakfast?"

"Planning on staying the night?" Linda asked.

"The worst thing about just taking a shower," Jessie smiled, "is when you realize that you're just going to get dirty again."

NINE
Jessie's Bad Date

Another Saturday night and I ain't got
nobody. I got some money 'cause I just got
paid. How I wish I had someone to talk to,
I'm in an awful way.
                    —*Another Saturday Night*, Sam Cooke

"Mr. Walker? Sorry to disturb you, but this is Patrick at the front desk. It seems there is a slightly *deshabille* young lady here asking for you."

Asking for me? As far as I knew, every woman who would come looking for me here already knew the way to my apartment.

"She seems, if you don't mind my saying… a little… distressed." His voice carried that sort of sense of understatement that desk clerks and hospital nurses adopt to reassure people that it might not be as bad as one thought. I hesitated for only a second or two.

"OK, I'll be down."

I guess I always had a weakness for damsels in distress. Besides, I wasn't really sure I had seen a woman who was slightly *deshabille*.

It was Jessie. She was not only *deshabille,* but also had a look of wide-eyed panic. She was breathing heavily and visibly shivering. Her right side stocking was torn and she was holding that shoe, with broken heel. Her blouse was intact, but askew. There was a tear at the hem of her skirt and even I could tell there was no way she deliberately arranged her hair in that array.

She didn't so much greet me as squeak loudly and wrap around my neck, sobbing quietly but energetically into my shoulder.

I half waved to the clerk as I guided her limping on one shoe toward the elevator. He shook his head with all the proper outrage and disapproval just barely perceptible—as a good desk clerk should.

"I'm sorry," she said, after I got her settled onto the couch and got a whisky into her. Considering the shape of her dress and all, I thought briefly that she might have already had a snootful, but it proved to do the trick as she began to slow down and breathe normally.

"What happened?"

"Oh…" she seemed startled that I asked, then hesitated dramatically, "it was… just a bad date."

I doubted it was as simple as that. Considering how hysterical she was when she arrived, and the condition of her clothes, she was at least understating the circumstances of this particular date.

"I came across with this guy I met. We went to that barbeque place over at the Tunnel, you know? We were having a nice time, and went down to the river, to… well, get better acquainted.

"Anyway, he got a bit too… frisky, you know, with his hands, so we struggled for a while until I got really mad and left."

That didn't make a lot of sense to me, either. As far as my experience went, Jessie had always been ready and willing in the "frisky" department. I was also pretty certain Jessie was smart enough to not get maneuvered into a corner like that, even if she wasn't interested in the guy.

"I remembered you lived here on the river, so I made my way over here. I managed to escape with my dignity somewhat intact anyway. As for my virtue, that had already been well accounted for, as you should know." She was vamping again… recovering from whatever fright she had earlier.

She moved closer to me and leaned up, inviting, even welcoming a kiss, leaving me wondering how she could shift from frightened by unwanted advances into being a bit aggressive and forward in such a short time. Apparently, it was only a temporary aversion to *frisky*. It could have been just my incredible sex appeal, but it had never seemed to overpower her, or anybody else, before.

Suddenly, another thought crossed my mind as she was kissing me.

"You left your purse behind?" I was a little surprised. On other occasions she seemed to be in her bag quite a bit, checking her makeup and the like. Come to think of it, she wasn't wearing her usual full complement of makeup.

"Oh, I... didn't bring one," she explained. "I had a lipstick in my jacket, which I left in his car. I only brought my drivers license and house key. I didn't want to fuss about a bag."

What woman would go out with a new fellow without full mask in place? It would make sense if she was the kind of girl who didn't use makeup or if she knew the fellow already, but normally on a first date, a girl like Jessie would put her best face forward, wouldn't she?

"Oh, my God," she said. "I must look awful. I didn't even bring a comb with me. Is it OK if I use yours?"

She went upstairs and used my hairbrush to restore some semblance of order and washed the smudges from her face as I stood at the bathroom door.

"You want to spend the night here?" I offered.

"I... could you just take me home instead? I mean I know it's late and I'm asking a lot, but I guess I'll just feel safer if I was back in my own bed, you know. I'd be willing to let you keep me company..."

It was about 2:30 in the morning, but tomorrow was Sunday and I hadn't planned on going to church, anyway. Besides, I really thought she might tell me what happened, perhaps over breakfast in the morning. *Not to mention that damsel thing I mentioned.*

"Sure, I suppose I could do that."

"You're a prince, Bradley."

Well, I'm a something, anyway.

As we exited on the Detroit side of the tunnel, she had snuggled into the crook of my arm. She stretched languidly when we got to the customs booth. Just another romantic couple crossing the border after a cozy evening. They passed us easily through and we were off toward Dearborn.

As we got to her place, I noticed a light on and a car in the driveway.

"Expecting company?" I said.

"It's just my brother," she explained. "He comes by sometimes to check on me. He has his own key. Probably already asleep."

The door swung open while I was pulling in. Apparently her brother stayed up.

"I'll just drop you off," I said.

"Don't be silly, the least I can do is offer you a nightcap. I insist."

The brother was not much taller than she was, about 5'8" or so. He had one of those wiry builds that suggested he had been an athlete. He was dressed in striped pajamas and a red silk bathrobe.

"Hey, Sis, you were out late." He said, as we entered the house. He seemed a lot more relaxed about the hour and my presence than I think I would have been if I had a sister, even at her place.

"Joey... you haven't been waiting up for me, have you?" she teased. "Because if you haven't heard, your sister is a big girl and doesn't need you to check up on her."

You could hear a bit of anger in her voice as well as playfulness. Obviously, they'd had this argument before.

"Look, I was out this way and thought I'd stay the night here. I'm not interfering."

"Oh, sure," she said with sarcasm. "Just in the neighborhood."

"I had a limo run for a guy in Ann Arbor and didn't feel like driving on home. I figured you could put me up for the night, but I'll keep going..."

"Oh, don't be silly, besides, you're already in your jammies," she said as she walked over to the kitchen.

"Hey, I'm Joe," he offered a hand.

"Brad Walker."

"CKLW! I know the voice. I like the music you guys play."

"What are you drinking, Brad?" Jessie's voice came from the kitchen.

"Beer if you've got it."

"Glass?"

"O.K."

She rattled glasses and ice trays.

"Brad saved my life tonight."

"What?"

"I just brought her home," I clarified.

"I was over in Windsor and got stranded. Bradley here, rescued me."

Joe's eyes narrowed a bit but then he smiled again. "I'm glad you got her home," he said, "Listen, I think I'll get some sleep, and I'm sure you two want some privacy. It was good meeting you Brad... 'Night, Sis."

Jessie handed me my drink.

"Don't worry," she said. "Joey just worries about me since our folks died. I love him, but I just can't resist teasing, or shocking, him sometimes. He's used to it by now."

If you say so.

I just stayed for the beer and a little kissing, but it was still almost the crack of dawn by the time I left.

As I walked to my car, I looked over at the limousine in the carport, obviously the one Joe was driving. But if Jessie had a date drive her to Windsor... where was *her* car?

TEN

A stunned nation.

06 June-68

Los Angeles (UPI)—New York senator Robert Kennedy was pronounced dead at Central Receiving Hospital at 12:17 am. Sen. Kennedy was expected to be the Democratic nominee for president. The senator was shot at the Ambassador Hotel…

I slept in on Thursday morning, getting across the street just in time to hit the air, only to find Charlie in the bullpen sprawled across two chairs almost directly under the jocks' message board, which read:

```
America        2
Kennedys       0
```

I seemed to need a moment to process.

"Bobby?"

"Yep, bastard shot him in a hotel kitchen after his speech. The good news, I suppose, is they tackled him on the spot. Fella named Sirhan, I think. Far as anybody knows… just another head case."

"We've been all news all morning," he continued. "Don't know when we're going back on the air. Chucklehead's been in and out of here a half-dozen times. Probably don't know whether to wind his watch or wipe his ass.

"In fact, I'll bet he's off winding his ass right now."

I could imagine Charlie coming in this morning, all wound up to hit the air only to be shunted aside for the news. He needed an audience and a chance to rant, and I was it.

"I guess I better go talk to Chuckles," I said turning back toward the door. Then stopped.

"Charlie… that sign…"

"Hey, what's faster than a speeding bullet… sure as hell ain't any Kennedy."

I left shaking my head.

"Where the hell have you been?"

"I believe I start at nine, Fred."

"But... alright, alright. We're thinking of going back to music in another hour or so, but I'm wondering... should we play anything special? I guess I was wondering if you had any suggestions."

Fred knew I had done some programming in my earlier stops and sometimes would ask for 'suggestions'. Of course, by the time any of my suggestions came through they had unquestionably become all his.

"I don't think we want to play anything special, but there's no question we might want to drop some of the psychedelic stuff, keep to straightforward music. We also really need to drop the jingles, and features, for now. Nice and subdued, simple."

It was sensible and reasonable, and I'm sure the station's programming gurus on the West Coast would feel *Fred* had made a good choice.

I went upstairs to the newsroom to see if there was anything I could do to lend a hand.

Mike LaSalle was mostly the afternoon news man, but the circumstances brought him in early. We had met in Fort Wayne, where I was just starting, while he was leaving for a job in Buffalo.

"Hey, Walker," he said, looking up from his typewriter. "Just getting in? There's a whole pile of wire copy over there." He gestured to a wire basket full of paper ripped from the teletype. "If you're looking for the boss..."

"Yeah, I know, I heard he and Mac were in the studio."

"Too bad it's all Kennedy today, we had a great story."

CKLW's 20/20 news (20 after the hour, 20 before the hour) was characterized by sensational details, dramatic announcers, and clever writing all done to the insistent staccato undercurrent of a teletype machine. The best stories were ones with a visual component that lent itself to memorable descriptive language with an emotional element that the announcer could really work with.

"...fisherman caught a floater in the river on the Detroit side. Detroit police are still withholding the name, but apparently she was blonde, good-looking..."

I nodded. It was the kind of thing that would promote a visceral reaction in the listeners. It was easy to put yourself in the shoes of the horrified angler.

"I see what you mean. I can imagine several possibilities... catch of the day... hooked a real beauty... latched onto a girl... stringing her along. It's a catchy story Mike."

"Ouch, I guess I set that up."

"I'm just saying it has *reel* potential."

"Enough already," he said, chuckling. "Time to throw a net over this thing."

"Don't worry, Mike, you guys are sure to work it in before the day is over."

> *(Sound of teletype) It's twenty minutes before 3, I'm Mike LaSalle, C—K—L—W, 20... 20... news... A local fisherman caught much more than he expected this morning when he reeled in a dead body. A beautiful young woman landed on the bank with death in her sightless eyes. The horrified angler hastily notified Police who tell us the foul corpse had been in the Detroit River for several days. Police are withholding identity of the victim until next of kin are notified...*

Even if I had heard the news reports, I would still have been unprepared for what I was to learn from the two men facing me in the hallway after my air shift ended.

One was short and squat. Not fat, exactly, but a stocky man with a wide profile. The other was taller than my 6'2"—pretty close to 6'6", I guess, and thin enough to seem almost stretched like a cartoon character.

"Are you Brad Walker?"

"At least three hours a day," I said, a bit sarcastically.

"Detective Sergeant Bryce McGowan, RCMP," the taller cop flashed his card. "This is Sgt. Joseph Talbert of the Detroit police."

"O...kay," I said.

"Is there a quiet place we can talk?"

I thought for a second and decided if it was going to be trouble, I'd rather not have it there.

"How about my apartment? It's just across the street."

The Mountie looked at the cop, who shrugged.

"Sure, why not?"

ELEVEN
A visit from the police

Just call me angel of the morning…..
—*Angel of the Morning*, Merrilee Rush

"Your full name, for the record?" The RCMP sergeant, McGowan, asked.

"Thomas Jefferson Chandler, Jr.…"

"Christ!" The Detroit cop, Talbert really could speak. A bit high pitched for a guy his size, but a good clear voice, with maybe a hint of Upper Peninsula Scandinavian influence.

"Brad Walker is… I guess you'd call it a stage name." I finished, then waited.

"What can I do for you gentlemen?" I finally asked.

"Do you know a Jessica Royce?"

Jessie? What the hell did she do this time?

"Yeah, I know Jessie." I said. "Has something happened to her?"

"How would you characterize your relationship with her?"

"Well, we went out a few times, with some mutual friends."

"Would that include Charles Kelly and," Talbot flipped his notebook, "Linda… Stevenson?"

"Right, Linda and Jessie were friends, Charlie and I are friends. We met a few weeks ago and got together a couple of times socially."

"You saw her on the night of 25th of last month, is that correct?"

"The other Saturday. Yeah, she came by here. Again what are we talking about here?"

"Have you heard from Mrs. Royce since then?"

MRS. Royce? I think I twitched a bit. You would think somewhere she might have mentioned a husband in the conversation. I don't know if it would have made a difference, but it just would have been nice to know.

"I have not. Is there a point here?"

"She's dead." Talbert watched me closely, waiting for a reaction, I suppose.

"The dead girl in the river?" I choked.

His eyes narrowed even more suspiciously. "What do you know about that?"

"I work at a radio station, remember? The floater fit her general description so it seemed a fair possibility when you come asking questions."

I looked a bit more closely at him. "So you're telling me she's been missing since the morning of May 26th?"

Talbert didn't answer, but fired a question of his own.

"Do you have any reason to believe she might have been involved in anything illicit—drugs perhaps?"

Drugs… I thought back to the party and what she had said to Linda…

"Drugs? No, I can't say I ever saw her using any drugs."

I decided not to mention her comment at the party because it didn't really mean anything, but might have caused trouble for Linda, who I liked. I sort of thought drugs didn't add up, anyway. If Jessie was hooked on anything, it would have had to be sex, not drugs.

"She wasn't even a heavy drinker. Why do you think she was involved with drugs?"

I could see the Mountie watching the cop—wondering how he was going to respond.

"I'll ask the questions," he answered gruffly.

As we glared at each other, the phone rang.

"You want to answer that?" Talbert asked.

I was tempted to let the front desk answer and take a message, the advantage of living in a hotel, but I answered it.

"That dead girl was Jessie!" Mac said excitedly without any of the usual preamble. "You know, the floater in the river. They haven't given any autopsy results, yet, but they…"

"Yeah, Mac, the police are here," I said. "They just told me."

He calmed a bit. "Oh. Look, I'm sure it's probably just routine."

"I'm not too certain about that." I supposed the cop could have just been an asshole, but I got a definite bad feeling from him.

"Really! Do you know something? Is there a story?"

"No, nothing like that. I'll tell you later. Listen, I don't want to keep the police waiting. I'll see you when you get home."

"Sure, Brad... I'll find out what I can learn here from the Detroit cops."

"OK, see ya' newshound." I hung up.

"Newshound?" Talbert asked.

"My roommate, Mac McCarthy, he's a newsman at the station."

The Mountie grinned. "The voice."

"Yeah."

I walked to the window and looked out toward the river. *What had happened to Jessie? Accident? Suicide?*

"Was she on this side, or that side, when she went in?"

"Still determining that," Talbert said gruffly.

"I'm afraid I don't know much that would help you, guys... poor Jessie. There was the incident that night, though... you know, the 25th."

I told them the story of Jessie's misadventure, including the fact that I never bought her bad date story. They seemed unsurprised, making me wonder if they suspected some kind of foul play. As I spoke, I continued to stare out toward the river.

I usually liked looking out at the river, seeing it as peaceful and calm, the few boats on the water just easing along. Today it seemed busy and crowded and dangerous. It was going to be a long time before I saw the river the way I used to... if ever.

"You were close? To the Royce woman?" Talbert asked.

"Not really, I mean, we were mostly a foursome and I was..."

"You had set your sights on the other girl... Linda?" McGowan asked.

"Yeah, you could put it that way. I certainly spent much more time talking with her than with Jessie. I mean, it seemed everyone liked her, she was in good spirits. Even after whatever happened that night, she didn't strike me as a person who could get distressed enough to jump into the river. Did she jump into the river? I can't see her out there swimming..."

"We're still investigating," Talbert said gruffly. He had that suspicious look again. "Do you know any of her family or friends?"

Charlie might know something, but he was already on Talbert's list and there was no need for me to point in his direction.

"Just the brother, Joe, who I mentioned and Linda. Hell, I didn't even know Jessie was married. The truth is… I'm not really certain I knew Jessie."

Or Linda, for that matter.

TWELVE
Comparing notes

Why does it do the way it does? Baby, how'd
we ever get this way
        —*Baby, How'd We Ever Get This Way*, Andy Kim

The cops asked several of the questions over again, hoping for better answers, maybe. After they left, I called Linda, in case she hadn't heard the news. She had also already spoken to the police.

"I hadn't seen her for several days," she said, "but that wasn't really that unusual. Sometimes, she'd disappear—I wouldn't see, or hear from her for several weeks, then she'd call me and we would hang out for several days running. You just never knew with her."

"When was the last time you saw her?"

"Last week, Sunday. Not last Sunday I mean, but the one before... the 26th I think. I was a bit surprised. She wanted to buy me dinner."

"Any particular reason?"

"She didn't mention any... Come to think of it the whole thing was a bit weird. Normally, if we got together for dinner, we split the bill. Sometimes I would treat her if things got a bit tight... or maybe when the restaurant was really expensive, you know?"

I knew. Linda worked because her father thought it was a good idea for a young woman to have her own income. Jessie worked to survive.

"She was behaving a bit strange, too. In most cases, she would be playful and flirting with every guy in sight. This time she was quiet. It was really just us..."

I heard her beginning to sob gently on the other end of the phone.

"Hey... hey... are you OK?" I said. "I didn't mean to bring up a lot of sad memories. Do you need me to come over? Maybe you shouldn't be alone."

"I don't know... later... maybe you could come by tonight?"

"Sure. I'll be there whenever you want me."

"I'll always want you." She said, her voice brightening a bit. "Brad..."

"Yeah,"

"Did the police give you any idea what happened to her? How she was drowned?"

"Not really. If the police thought she had killed herself, I would have thought they would ask more questions about how she was behaving, how her spirits were, and stuff like that."

"But what else could it be? Nobody swims in the Detroit River for fun..."

"...And if she had fallen off a boat, you'd think someone would have reported it."

"By the way, Brad, you didn't tell the police about that little joke Jessie told the other week—at the party—you know, the one about coke..."

"No, I didn't mention it."

Although I found myself wondering, more and more, why? Who was I protecting? Jessie was already dead and needed no protection from secrets. I had little concern for Joe, her brother. I had thought a bit of Linda, but the only reason to protect her would be if she was involved in the same drug business that might have killed her friend.

I had been trying to convince myself that there had been nothing to her declaration about having a source for cocaine, but the note of concern in Linda's voice proved she never read it as a joke, and whoever Jessie might have gotten drugs from might easily have killed her... something I should have maybe told the cops.

Either way, I was beginning to suspect Linda definitely knew more than she was letting on.

"Is it OK if I changed my mind?" She asked. "About coming over right away... Maybe the sooner the better?"

"On my way."

*It's 9 o'clock at the big 8 as we get ready for another
million dollar weekend! Let's open with the Doors, light it up
baby!"*
Song: *Light My Fire*

"Poor Jess."

"I can't believe it Charlie, I just saw her a little over a week
ago."

"Yeah, Jess told me she had been to see you," he drawled.
"She was a busy girl the last few weeks. She saw *you* that
Saturday, me, that Sunday, and I hear she did Chucklehead in
your shower the other week."

I hadn't mentioned her little escapade to him, but wasn't that
surprised word had gotten back to him. He looked at me with a
slight grin, but I couldn't really tell if he was amused or a little
disappointed.

"By the way, where were you that night of the party?"

I had been curious, and since we were on the subject...

"Oh, I had things to do," he said, vaguely.

Things to do?

"Apparently, so did she."

"So she did."

We lapsed into silence. Our own personal "dead air".

I did a quick announce into The Temptations' "I Wish it
Would Rain" which then led into Mac's 20/20 newscast.

"So it must have been some kind of accident," Charlie said.

"I suppose."

"Cops ask you a lot of questions?"

"I don't know, mostly routine stuff. They did ask if she was
involved with drugs."

"Nah, with Jess it would have to be men."

I nodded.

"The cops don't think it's suicide, do they?"

"I don't think so, I think they would have asked different
questions."

Charlie paused.

"You don't think they suspect us of anything, do you?"

Suspect us? Of what?

"Well, they wouldn't tell you if they did, would they?" I
answered. "Besides, they're going to be disappointed if they do,
since we really don't know anything."

Charlie nodded.

The news ended and I led into the "Blast From The Past." The number one song from that date in 1959: "Kansas City," by Wilbert Harrison .

I had barely clipped the mic, when Mac strolled into the studio.

"What the hell did that girl get you guys into, Walker?" He asked.

I had spent the night at Linda's so Mac and I never got a chance to compare notes about our conversations with the police.

"What do you mean, Mac?"

"My police sources say she was probably strangled," he said laconically.

"Strangled?" Charlie squawked.

"Well, it has to be confirmed, of course, but it kind of looks like she was killed first, then dumped in the river, probably weighted down to keep her from being discovered for several days."

"Holy shit," Charlie said.

"Best guess is from at or near the Detroit side, but pinpointing the dump site is going to be very tricky."

"Who the hell would kill Jessie?" I wondered.

We looked at each other.

"Jealous boyfriend?" Charlie said with a grin.

"You confessing, Charlie?" I grinned back.

"I was thinking Chuckles."

I laughed out loud.

"I was just thinking," Charlie said, "since she blew his… mind, maybe he blew a fuse, too."

"Not a chance!" I answered. "He might be an absolute asshole, but he couldn't kill anyone… without fucking up."

We were all laughing. As if it helped us make any sense of it.

"Poor kid." I finally said.

"You guys OK?" Mac asked solicitously. "I mean I know you didn't know her for long, but you guys seemed pretty close."

"It's really kind of strange," I said. "I keep thinking that I don't really know her, but I clearly had feelings for her. Right now, I'm more worried about Linda. She and Jessie were very close, and she's really struggling."

Charlie said nothing, he seemed miles away in thought. I wondered if he was OK.

"Well, I'll keep digging out what I can from the cops." Mac said. "If there's anything else I can do for you guys, just let me know."

"This is really starting to look like a long, strange, trip," Charlie finally said.

Thirteen
The Drug Kingdom

```
   I am the god of hellfire and I bring you…
Fire, I want you to burn…  Fire, I want you to
learn.
                        —Fire, Arthur Brown
```

(Jingle) More music… C—K—L—W
It's 11:27 at the big 8 with Brad Walker diggin some Motown.
Here's Marvin and Tammy, 'Ain't Nothing Like the Real Thing'.
(music)

Charlie stuck his head into the studio as the song came up.

"Armand needs to see us," he said. "Today. He says it's urgent."

"Urgent! What the hell does he do that's any kind of an emergency? I mean promotion and producing doesn't really call to mind 'urgency' does it?"

Charlie shook his head with a half shrug. "All I can tell you Brad, is that he seemed to believe it's an emergency and he wants to see us. We might as well drop over there. I figure we can take the 'Vette."

His grin was obvious when he finished. The station was giving away a Red '68 Corvette Sting Ray to the person who could guess the exact mileage on the car. We all took turns driving it so long as we called in a mileage check every three hours.

They never gave us any limit to how far we could drive, and I have to admit I was always tempted to cruise on down to Toledo in the thing and shock hell out of the old neighborhood.

Charlie had a point. Why not find out just what an 'urgent' meeting constituted? It wasn't like I had other things to do, and knowing Armand, it would all end in free food or drink.

We ended up leaving the station just after noon, taking the longer route over the bridge in defiance of the 'urgency' of his call.

There were a couple of white Chrysler Imperials parked in the lot next to Armand's blue '62 Thunderbird.

Charlie and I looked at each other. "Investors," we chorused.

Armand had a habit of setting up these kind of 'accidental' meetings between us and local music groups, investors, or other people important to him, like visiting record company executives. The idea was to show them that he had access to local radio hosts. We were important at C K because we played more of the soul groups he tended to represent.

"Hey," Charlie said, "Isn't that one guy the 'Ice Cream Man'? From the Stag House?"

I nodded. "I think so."

We walked into the studio and found Armand in conversation with a well-dressed black man about my age. He wore his hair trimmed in the older, pre-Afro, style and had a pencil thin mustache. I became certain he was the fellow that was wearing a white suit at Armand's Stag Club dance. There were half a dozen other men in the studio with them. As we walked into the studio the men fanned out into a line facing us.

Armand looked ill.

"I'm very sorry, my friends," he said. "I really had no choice."

Charlie and I looked at each other.

"Gentlemen," the dapper man said. "I'm terribly sorry for the deception that we used to get you here, but I assure you we only need a few minutes of your time."

"Which of you is Mr. Walker?"

I was perplexed, but I shrugged. "That would be me." I paused for a moment. "What's this all about?"

"My name is Bobby Charlton," he said, as if that should have meant something. These are my associates, Matthew, Mark, Luke, and John."

He introduced the four men nearest to him. I smiled and nodded at the names, and wondered if his name was also invented. I was beginning to also wonder what happened to Armand's silent partner, Bennie.

"I see we have a bible scholar here," he chuckled.

"I've been to church a few times," I agreed. Like many people I went often as a kid, but had stopped attending when I moved out on my own.

The two fellows at either end of the line clearly deserved no introduction, which, ironically, had me paying more attention to them. One was an older man, early 40's, stocky build about 5'8 or 5'9. The other was a skinny little fair skinned black kid who looked about fourteen or fifteen.

"If you gentlemen will excuse us," Charlton said politely to Armand and Charlie, "I'd like to have a private word with Mr. Walker on a business matter."

Armand dropped his head. "I'm very sorry, my friend. Very sorry."

"Sorry?" I asked.

"I tried to stop them…"

At this point a couple of the 'associates' began herding Armand and Charlie toward the door.

"Now wait a damned minute," Charlie interjected, stepping toward Charlton. The older guy flashed a pearl-handled Colt revolver in a holster under his coat.

"Easy, gentlemen," Charlton said coolly, "no one needs to get hurt here. If you would please just wait for your friend outside, we will have a polite, *but private*, conversation and you will all be free to go."

"What the hell is this, Armand? Who is this guy?" Charlie had turned to Armand.

"I had no choice. I'm sorry"

"You said that already!" I challenged. Knowing he would add nothing.

This didn't make much sense. Sure, *Armand* dealt with a few questionable characters, but what did I have to do with any of that? What was the hold this Charlton had over Armand and what did they think I could do for them? I had been dropped squarely into the soup. It would have been nice to know something, instead of being led in deaf, blind, and stupid.

Charlie backed away toward the door, his eyes as wide as saucers. The gunman began to steer Armand toward the door. I met eyes with Charlie, but there was little we could do for each other at that point.

"John, please make sure our friends don't do anything rash like make a run for it, or call for the police, won't you?"

"Solid," he answered, heading off toward the door.

Of the remaining henchmen, Mark and Luke began to flank me on either side, as I began to swivel my head, getting more nervous.

"What's this all about?" I asked.

"It's about your girlfriend who went swimming the other week."

"Jessie?"

"Your girlfriend was taking care of a little package for us. Since she is, well... no longer available, we figure you might know where it is?"

"Why would I know where it is? What kind of package are you talking about?"

"Oh, just a few keys," Mark said, "you know, a little taste?"

Drugs. Maybe the cops were right about their suspicions. Jessie was involved in some kind of drug business and this Charlton clearly thought *I* knew something.

Maybe the night Jessie showed up was a drug deal gone bad. She must have run off with the drugs or the money and they thought I knew what she did with it.

"She wasn't exactly my girlfriend... we only went out a couple of times."

I looked over my shoulder again but the two 'gospels' were already grabbing me, pinning my arms behind my back.

"I hear you saw her right after she got the package," he said. "I figure she must have left it with you."

Who would have told them that I was that close to Jessie, especially since it wasn't true?

"Me? We barely knew each other!" I argued excitedly. "Why would she leave anything valuable with someone she knew only a few weeks?"

Charlton looked at me skeptically. I knew the cops didn't believe me, but it was even scarier with this bunch.

"I don't know who told you *I* knew something, but Jessie was just a friend. She didn't tell me anything, she never gave me anything... Hell, she never even told me she was married!"

Charlton shrugged, then gestured to the little guy who stepped up and hit me.

He would have made a pretty good welterweight fighter, because I barely saw his hands move. I'm no athlete anyway, but with my arms pinned behind me, my rib cage was just like one of those heavy training bags. The one-two was a straight punch to the gut followed quickly by a left hook into the short ribs. The pain was intense enough to make me scream, if only I could have drawn in enough air.

The pair holding me had no trouble switching from keeping me in place to holding me up.

"Now Brad… You don't mind me calling you Brad, do you?" Charlton hit me with a reptilian grin. "I would never suggest you were lying to me, but are you sure you didn't just sort of forget that the girl left you something?"

I shook my head as emphatically as I could. "No," I barely croaked.

I got another hook to the ribs.

"You really don't want to see how the kid works on faces," he said.

The little guy gave me one more to the gut for emphasis, and the two thugs let me drop while the last of the air rushed out of me. I landed on hands and knees, until the one on my left side kicked me in the other, previously un-abused, rib cage—just to balance me out, I guess.

"Brad, I just wouldn't want to think that if you happened to find my little package that you might give it to someone else, or even worse, try to go into business for yourself."

"I don't know," I gasped for air, "anything about any of this."

"That is a very sensible attitude, Brad. Even if you were to return my package to me, you should continue to live by that philosophy."

A couple of his henchmen chuckled. A chill tried to run down my spine, but never got through the pain.

I don't think I passed out exactly, but the next thing I was aware of was Charlie leaning over me.

"How you doing, buddy?"

"Hurts like hell," I groaned.

Armand was hovering nearby. "I am sorry. I had no choice."

"Will you stop saying that!"

I used so much of my air to shout at him, it ended in a fit of coughing, which was even more painful.

"We'd better get you to a hospital," Charlie said.

"No," Armand said, "when they see his injuries they will involve the police who will bring trouble for us all."

"What the hell do you think we're in now, Armand? They kidnap us at gunpoint, break poor Brad's ribs… we need all the police protection we can get."

I was trying to gingerly find my bruised ribs to make sure they were still there. "He's right," I said in a perfect imitation of a stage whisper. "No police. That Detroit cop already thinks I'm involved in Jessie's death. This beating would just make me suspect number 1."

"But Brad, you could have a broken rib or a punctured lung!"

"I don't know, they seem OK. If I'm still having trouble later, we'll worry then."

Charlie shook his head. "*I* could at least use a drink." He said.

"You are right," Armand said, "I owe you fellows several drinks each."

"Not to mention," I croaked, "a fucking explanation."

FOURTEEN
Complications and Explanations

...laugh about it, shout about it, when you
have to choose, any way you look at it you
lose.
                    —*Mrs. Robinson*, Simon and Garfunkel

Armand led us to a small, hole-in-the-wall bar just a couple of blocks down the street from the studio. The building (painted orange) sat back from the corner, with angled spaces along the long wall of the building for cars to park.

Charlie stopped to call in a mileage report to the radio station from the pay phone that sat at the street corner. Armand and I walked into the bar. The door at the front side opened into a set of four booths down the short side under the light of high windows. The bar ran along the opposing side. In the middle, a few tables occupied the near ground, while a raised floor held a pool table with two middle aged men silently, but rapidly playing. It reminded me of Morrie's Tavern in my neighborhood back home.

The half dozen men in the bar ranged between about 40 and 60 plus, all of them black. They looked at us coming in with a mixture of surprise and curiosity. I found myself wondering if we might have been the first white people who had ever been in the place. I smiled a bit as I eased myself gingerly into a chair at the nearest table.

The bartender was a wiry sort of fellow whose tired eyes and scarred face suggested he was probably an ex-fighter. He just stepped out from behind the bar.

"Help you gents," he said, without facial expression.

"Beer... three beers," Armand said.

The barman nodded. "Pabst Blue Ribbon?"

"OK, and I think a whisky for my friend." He indicated me.

I hated whisky, but I figured it would take effect quickly and ease the pain faster than the beer. I nodded. "Scotch."

Charlie had caught up with us by the time he returned with a tray holding three bottles of beer and three water glasses, as well as a squat glass with liquor in it.

I drained the glass slowly, the burn of liquor warming my sore ribcage, just a little.

"Perhaps now, you can explain what that was all about?" I said.

He hung his head. "I'm sor…"

He caught my eye, then restarted. "I feel terrible, my friends, it was only supposed to be a friendly chat. They promised me in so many words that no one would get hurt."

"Well, I think Brad, here, might have a bit of a disagreement with them on that," Charlie fumed. "Who the hell were those guys?"

"They were drug runners," I explained. I filled them in on the 'conversation' I had with Charlton. As I described the encounter I got a bit enthusiastic and made the mistake of attempting to demonstrate the punch that hit me.

"I suppose guys like that might only count something that caused permanent damage as harm," I said, trying to smile, "But I wouldn't want to bet my life on any assurance that a gangster might give me. The real question is: How did any of us get involved with this?"

Armand seemed to become a human shrug. "They came into the office and told me to get you here or they would hurt me."

"…and you figured better us than you," Charlie muttered. "You should have waited and made sure they were serious first."

"It was just supposed to be a talk." He answered petulantly.

"So where was Bennie?" The question had crossed my mind earlier, but had gotten lost in my subconscious. A guy Bennie's size might have helped even the odds a bit.

"Dentist's appointment."

Convenient, I thought.

"How did they know to reach us, no make that me, through you, Armand?"

His eyes dashed between us quickly, then sought a higher location.

"I don't know," he lied.

"Don't give me that. You knew who these guys were when they walked in today—we were the ones who learned that the hard way. Now, how did they know to look for me, and what do you know about Jessie Royce?"

Charlie jumped up, his chair dropping to the floor, grabbing Armand by his lapels.

"What! You knew Jessie? What the hell is going on here Armand?"

"Hold it! I don't know any Jessie!" He spluttered. "I didn't tell them anything... they told *me* to find you two. I didn't get any reasons."

"Easy, Charlie," I said. I felt the pain as I jumped up, but had the good sense to raise my left hand to reach across the table.

"We're drawing an audience," I remarked.

The pool game has stopped and the barman was headed toward us.

"Everything OK, gentlemen?" He asked politely.

"Sure," I answered, "just a little argument."

"Oh, yes," Armand said, "just a disagreement between good friends."

Charlie released him, then slumped into his seat, putting his face into his hands.

"Don't want no troubles," the barman said.

"How does Charlton know you and how did he know to use you to find me?"

"I was working with a singing group out of Toledo that called themselves the Mercurys."

I exploded a laugh, prompting another bout of coughing and more pain.

"What's so damned funny?" Charlie asked.

"The Mercurys were the original name of our hockey team in Toledo."

They both looked back blankly. I have to admit; even I didn't know why I found that particularly funny.

"Well, anyway, Charlton was introduced to me as one of their backers. He showed up at several of their concerts and recording sessions. Then I hit a bit of a rough patch and needed money. Charlton offered me good terms so I took it."

"Don't tell me, you didn't manage to pay him back."

"Well there were a couple of setbacks."

"Jesus, Armand..." Charlie exclaimed.

"As the pressure built, I eventually had to let him have a piece of my company."

I nodded. "Just out of curiosity, Armand, how much of your company do you still own?"

Our eyes met and I saw my question hit home with him. He had parceled out most if not all of his company to his creditors. He gave me a snake-oil salesman smile, but never mentioned a figure.

"So your 'investor' just drops by from time to time as the mood strikes him and today he just came by and decided he wanted me set up?"

"I do not know why he wanted me to call you fellows. I do not know how he would know this Jessie girl, my friends. Charles mentioned the girl to me when we talked today, but only that you knew her. Are you sure Charlton didn't know the girl?"

"Even if he did, how did he link Brad with her?" Charlie asked. "And more importantly, why didn't he ask me any questions. I spent more time with her than Brad."

"Maybe the cops were right about Jessie being involved and she was supposed to be smuggling something to the Canadian side of the border for this Charlton. That would explain why he thought I had it."

"Perhaps he found out about you from this Jessie. You met her at the Stag House, right? Maybe she met Charlton there."

"...and then told him about me when they started doing business together?" I followed his logic. "It doesn't make a lot of sense that way. I wasn't involved with them."

"But if he was keeping an eye on her that night..." Charlie argued.

"Then they would already know where to look for this packet. She didn't have anything with her when she got to me. She must have already stashed it or given it to someone. Somebody had to point to me."

Armand shook his head. "Oh, no, my friend! I did not know enough to, as you say, point. You must look elsewhere."

Elsewhere? *Charlie?* I mean, he knew both Jessie and Armand, knew about that misadventure... but he also knew that I would have told him if she had left something didn't he? He had to know I would confide in him. I trusted him.

I dismissed the idea as simply paranoid. Charlie couldn't have been involved. OK, even if he was part of the smuggling ring, he would have had better ways of dealing with me.

Either way, I wasn't going to learn anything more that day.

We fell silent around the table.

"C'mon Brad," Charlie, my friend, said. "I'll take you home."

FIFTEEN
Another Meeting

I've been waiting so long, to be where I'm
going, in the sunshine of your love.
                    —*Sunshine of Your Love,* Cream

It was a beautiful Saturday, so I decided to call my friend
Casey Pierson and barbeque for her and her kids out in Grosse
Pointe Woods. I was hoping it would keep me from puzzling
over Jessie's death.

I had thought she was joking about wanting to smuggle
drugs, but what if she was—was she killed by her partners? Or
maybe the competition? Bobby Charlton seemed to suggest she
might have been involved in a deal, but maybe he had killed her
and was just working a smokescreen to get us to drop our guard.
Could Charlie have been involved? I mean he'd seen her a
couple of times more than I did. Come to think of it, there was
that shower thing back at the apartment with Chucklehead Fred.
Could they have kept seeing each other?

Mac's source at the Detroit Police told him that she was
probably killed on the Detroit side of the river. If the motive
wasn't crime, wouldn't it have to be jealousy? Her husband was
still in Vietnam, and obviously she didn't have a habit of telling
the other guys about him, but what if somebody else was
involved with her, and found out about Charlie or I. We knew
about each other, of course, but we were OK with that, I think.

Casey and I started our "affair" when we worked together in
Fort Wayne while she was getting a divorce. She was now
working as a Montessori pre-school teacher, no longer in radio.
I had stayed with her, off and on, until April when Dr. King was
shot and I moved to Windsor.

"Poor Jeff," Casey said when she saw me. "You look like
you haven't slept in a week."

"I'm OK, Casey." I gave a half-hearted smile to try to reassure her, but I certainly didn't mind her holding me close for a minute or so.

I was just about to drop the match on the charcoal when the doorbell rang.

"Somebody's at the door for you," she said, looking confused. There weren't a lot of people who knew how to get hold of me there and she *knew* them.

When I opened the door there was a guy about 5'9", dark hair, sort of standard build, dressed in a very nice navy blue suit, and a pair of very fancy shoes polished to a high sheen.

"Walker?"

"Who wants to know?"

"Listen," he said, opening his suit coat. "You don't want to alarm the lady or the kids... You just want to come with me. My boss wants to see you."

I hesitated, looking inside the coat flap at the handle of the pistol he was subtly showing me. My ribs began to ache again.

Oh great, more gangsters.

"Don't make this any worse," he said, almost as if he knew what I was thinking, "by trying to call the cops or making a run or something. We're just going to talk. If we wanted you dead, we'd have done this differently.

"On the other hand... if we have to kill you, don't think we won't."

"Can't we do this later?"

"Nobody keeps the boss waiting... if you don't want to end up landfill."

"Any idea how long..." I grinned a bit. "You know, so the folks here don't get worried."

"Shouldn't be more than a couple hours. Tell her I'm with the cops or something."

I looked him over. He didn't really look like a cop, but he wasn't obvious as a hood either. Besides, he was right. If we didn't want Casey running around playing Joan of Arc, I needed to reassure her, and she'd be less likely to call the police if she thought they had me in the first place.

"OK, be out in a minute."

The guy climbed into the back of the black Eldorado with me, as a guy who looked like an ex-prize fighter drove. It was a good idea to keep him in the car. The driver would have been first cast in Hollywood for the role of mob muscle.

"Matt Donovan," he said by way of introduction. I didn't answer.

"You're not from here, are you?"

"Ohio." I said, noncommittally.

Make him search the whole state (not that he wouldn't start with Toledo first).

"Then you might not know the old man. He started out with the Purple Gang, then slowly worked his way to the top of the organization…"

The Purple gang, rumrunners in the 20's, were so infamous, we had even heard of them back home. The Purples killed a popular Toledo bar owner because of a rumor he was going to spill the beans.

"…he's sort of retired these days, but took a personal interest in this dead girl.

"See, normally we wouldn't care—the organization doesn't deal in drugs. The old bosses still think selling drugs are more dangerous to society than booze or broads or gambling. They think the drugs are immoral. We leave that to niggers like Bobby Charlton, who runs the cocaine business or crooked cops like Mitchell Martin, who handles most of the Heroin trade."

Now I was genuinely confused. "But if Jessie was killed over drugs, what do you want from me?"

"Jessie is, I mean was, the old man's granddaughter."

"His granddaughter?" *Oh, shit! Nothing good's going to come out of this.*

"Look, we just went out a couple of times… I mean she spent most of the time…" Wait… did I want to get off the hook by putting Charlie on? Hell, they probably already had talked to Charlie. Besides, we all were just friends and we should have nothing to hide.

"Most of the time…" he prompted.

"Well, she was with her friend, Linda, and I was well, we were sort of a group together with my buddy… it was kind of all…"

"You had your eye on the other girl?"

"Listen, it was just a few times together… I don't know that any of us knew that much about each other."

"Did you know she was married?"

"Not until the cops told me last week."

"Did your buddy know?"

I shrugged. "Couldn't tell you. Wouldn't think so."

"Be honest, Walker, would it have mattered? I mean, we're men of the world here, right? I even heard rumors she was a hot piece."

I said nothing. I was raised to believe 'a gentlemen never tells' and who knew what would happen if they found out we had both made it with her, not to mention that little combination thing she seemed to enjoy so much.

"I suppose it doesn't really matter... unless the old man starts asking. Maybe it would be better to hope the subject doesn't come up, huh?"

We finished the ride in silence. I was surprised to find we ended up at the Detroit Institute of Art.

Again he anticipated the question. "Like I said, Walker, a friendly meeting. Nice public place. Just talk to the old man and you're free to go... I'll give you a lift back or you can take a cab if you're worried about us taking you for a ride."

His pantomime of a machine gun even got me to laugh. I might be able to survive this, I was thinking, but then I hadn't met the big boss, yet.

SIXTEEN
Trusting in Art

```
I feel it in my fingers, I feel it in my toes,
love is all around me…
            —Love is All Around, The Troggs
```

I was never introduced to the old man by name, but I later learned his name was Dino Colissimo. Mac and the other newsmen at the station referred to him as Mr. C.

I found him standing in the main courtyard of the museum looking at Diego Rivera's mural.

"Isn't this thing amazing?"

I nodded. "It's very impressive."

"You know, this Riviera was offered a bundle of money to paint one of these things for Rockefeller, you know. But Rockefeller put a stop to it when he found out that he was painting pictures of Lenin and Stalin and a bunch of commies on the thing. Why would the guy do that? Paint commies and stuff. Even if he was Commie, he had to know Rockefeller wouldn't ever put up with it, huh?"

It was a moment before it occurred to me he actually expected me to answer. I shrugged.

"I don't know," I began, "maybe he figured if he couldn't paint what he wanted to—even if it was Lenin—it really wasn't his work anyway. They should have gotten someone else."

"But Commie or not, he had to want the money, didn't he? Or he wouldn't have went to work for Rockefeller."

"Maybe it was because he valued the art more. It was important that people see the truth of what he painted."

"But nobody saw it!"

He had a point there, and I had run out of argument anyway, so I shrugged again. But then a thought came to me.

"Maybe he thought it was better to have people disturbed by the truth than just accept a lie."

"What about you, Walker? Are you an artist?"

I almost smiled. "I suppose not. I value the truth, but maybe not enough to risk everything."

"Smart kid," he said approvingly. "My people tell me you're on the radio?"

"Mid-mornings on CKLW."

He nodded a bit as if in recognition. "I've heard that station. I think you guys play way too much of that modern jungle jive jazz. I don't go for that... I don't mean the coloreds, just this loud new music they're playing. Some of those older guys played real music, not like these kids. Guys like Duke Ellington played classy stuff, elegant, you know. This new generation has passion, but not much style. As for that rock and roll stuff, they don't sing, they just twang guitars and screech."

I shrugged again. If they were going to have me killed it wouldn't be because I'd been playing Wilson Pickett.

"Then again, old people didn't like the music I listened to as a kid, either. If kids like it, that's what keeps the station going, right?"

"I play what they tell me." I said, trying not to sound defensive.

We looked at the mural in silence for what seemed like months.

"Listen," I finally said. "I don't know who killed Jessie. I don't know why... I didn't—still don't... know anything about the drug smuggling business, or how Jessie was involved in it. We were just friends! A bunch of us got together for dinner a couple of times."

"Drugs! Who said she was using drugs?"

"I don't know, the cops seemed to think she was involved with drugs, somehow."

"Idiots. Listen, son, the cops have drugs on the brain. There has to be another reason."

"Sure, I guess I just went with their assumption... I'm afraid I didn't know her very well."

"You were out with her a couple of weeks ago, when she got into trouble."

"Now wait a minute! I wasn't exactly out with her as much as she came to *me*. I just took her home."

I told the story of her late night visit and the story she told about the date. He asked me if I believed it and I explained again, that I was fairly certain she was lying, but had no way of investigating her story, nor anyway of forcing her to tell me the truth.

"There was gunfire along the river that night and the Canadian cops think it was a drug deal gone bad, so I guess they put two and two together."

"And got five."

"Maybe, but I think she might have known someone or something about some kind of drugs."

I mentioned what she said at the party, suggesting it was something I hadn't taken seriously. The truth was, I believe she intended to score coke, but chose to stay out of it. But if this was the deal that got her killed, that had to mean somebody at the station was also involved.

"What's with all this flitting around with her? Didn't you know she had a husband in Vietnam?"

He pronounced it as a two-syllable word (VEET nam).

"I never knew she had a husband anywhere until I heard it from the cops yesterday. She never wore any ring or anything and so we figured both she and her friend were unattached."

The old man fixed me with a withering glance.

"You use drugs?"

"No. I mean, I might have smoked a bit of grass on occasion..."

"No cocaine?"

"Never," I said. "I'm not looking to make a big score either. But then, if I was, I would probably lie under these circumstances."

He smiled gently.

"What can I say? I'm a DJ, not an artist. The truth is, I want you to find the bastard who killed Jessie as much as anybody. I just don't know how to start."

"If you learn anything, you'll tell us, right?"

"Sure."

"And you should probably stay clear of the cops. Oh, that's not a warning, son. I just think they might eventually find a frame that'll fit you."

"Me? I guess I knew they were suspicious..."

"Cops are like everybody else. They get paid for production. They need a killer... they'd like the guilty one, but they get paid the same either way. They ain't artists, they'll take the money."

"Well, surely some of them would be honest, wouldn't they?"

"Trust me, kid. It's my experience that the only cops that can't be bought are the ones in business for themselves."

SEVENTEEN
Understanding Family

Outside the museum, a Lincoln limousine had pulled in behind Donovan's Eldorado and the two drivers were sharing a laugh.

I knew who it was before I recognized Joe Landis in his chauffeur's uniform.

"Sorry to hear about your sister, Joe."

He shook my offered hand.

"We should talk," he said, without emotion. "I'll drive you back to Grosse Pointe."

Although I still harbored some suspicions about my original ride being something out of an old gangster movie, I wasn't sure this one didn't have even more danger. As one of the last known people to see Jessie alive, surely Joe would have to suspect I knew something, and if he thought I was involved in her death, he would probably want revenge.

On the other hand, there was no good way to decline without seeming even more suspicious. Also, I wanted to find out what happened to her as well, and Joe was the last person I knew that saw her. We really did need to talk.

"Yeah, OK," I answered.

I was the one with the first questions. "So how did you end up in the 'family' business, Joe? They told me you two weren't supposed to know about the organization?"

"Well, I hired in as a driver for the car service. I sort of stumbled across the mob connection on my own, but I still try to stay out. Neither my dad's parents, who raised us, nor Jessie ever knew I was working for an organization front. I stay to the legit side of the business—I get a W-2 and everything."

"That client from the other week? Was that your Grandfather?"

"Yeah, he goes out there every other week to see Mom."

"Jessie said your mom was dead."

"Insane," he said in a practiced tone. "Been locked up since we were little kids and Dad died. It was easier for dad's folks to tell us she was just dead. Then after we got old enough to know, there was still the question of how others tended to react."

I nodded understanding.

"She's in a private sanitarium just outside of Jackson. Dino, my grandfather, goes out every other week."

"That's how you found out about each other?"

"Yeah, I drove him a couple of times, then he started asking for me. I don't think he knew who I was at first, but we kept talking along the way and comparing notes, and we eventually learned who was who and what was what.

"He goes out Saturdays and stays and goes to Mass on Sunday, but I just can't feel comfortable when I stay overnight, so I come home, then run out to pick him up Sunday afternoon."

I understood. He was still struggling with the emotions stirred up by his mother's illness.

"That's why I always worried about Jess. I mean, she has... had... some kind of..."

He faltered.

"...well she had to have men. I don't mean... Look, there's nothing wrong with a woman having healthy urges, but with my sister it seemed... well, I always worried it was more of a sickness. When we were in school, she developed a reputation as a girl who was... well, always willing, so I was surprised when she married Matt Royce."

"He knew her reputation?"

"Sure, they were classmates, Jess was even caught 'at it' a couple of times. We all knew. There was a suggestion of locking her up, but Papa, my other Grandfather, was like me, and couldn't bear to see her end up like Mom.

"Look, Brad, I'm sorry if you thought you had an exclusive..."

"No, don't worry about that, Joe," I said, "we were barely friends. I never thought we had any exclusive. I was just surprised to learn she was married."

"She never acted like it. Matt married her just before he went overseas. She was pretty discreet about not, as far as I know, fooling around with his friends, but she was more or less business as usual." He smiled crookedly, "but you've been seeing her a while, right?"

"Me? I only met her about a month ago.

I was a little shocked to hear it when I put it in those terms. It did seem we were close, but perhaps that was because of the sexual connection. I had felt we knew each other, when in fact, I keep realizing I knew almost nothing.

Did I really want to get more involved? Certainly the cops or the family was much more capable of getting to the bottom of this better than I ever was going to be…

But then, maybe the old man was right, everybody needed a guilty party. Maybe it was just as easy to point at Brad Walker and declare the thing over, than track down an actual killer.

"…surprised because she spent a lot of time over in Windsor with somebody…"

"What was that?" I had apparently tuned Joe out while musing.

"She had spent a lot of time over the river in the last year or so."

"She told me she'd never been to Canada."

We drove on in silence for a moment. Me, resisting the urge to ask the question that he worked up the courage to answer before I asked.

"I really looked up to my big sister, but when I got old enough to realize how powerful those 'urges' of hers were, I started to keep an eye on her… I was worried about her getting into some kind of dangerous situation. I tried to stay out of sight, but she caught me pretty easy. After a while it became a game, her running around, me trying to keep tabs on her. In the meantime she used to tell me stories about her lovers, thinking I was enjoying that sort of thing, so I stopped following her."

"Then how do you know…"

"Old habits. There are still days I just can't resist."

"But she'd been seeing somebody in Canada for over a year?"

"At least."

"So we should look for a guy over there."

"One thing for sure… whatever trouble Jessie was in," he paused

"Yeah?"

"It's a sure bet there are a pair of pants attached."

That was good. We needed a chuckle. Joe turned on the radio (CKLW of course) and we traveled in silence.

"Joe?"

"Yeah."

"Did you see her at all after... that night?"

"Next morning. She fixed breakfast. Just like nothing happened. Did you buy that bad date story?"

"No. But, whatever happened to her, she was pretty freaked out. The more I think about that moment, the more I think someone might have tried to kill her."

"Why?"

"Timing, mostly. Something scares her one night, then a few days later she's dead. Conclusion: whatever scared her came back to kill her."

"I don't know, Brad, it's a bit thin."

"Thin or not, the question is: how did she get to Windsor that night?"

"Well, I assume she went with whoever she was running away from later."

"So where's *her* car?"

"Oh, that's a good question. If she drove over, why would she need a ride home, and if she didn't, where did she meet the guy who did?"

"Cops are probably looking as well, but maybe you can pass the word to the *family*. What is it anyway?"

"Her car?"

"Yeah, I don't think I ever saw it."

"Black '67 Mustang."

"Convertible, I suppose?"

"What else?"

"New car? What else did she do for a living?"

"Hey!"

"Hey, what? I just wondered if she had a second job."

"She was just working as a Kelly girl."

I shrugged, it just seemed a new car was a bit much on a Kelly girl's paycheck, but you never know.

"Good," I said, "maybe we can find out who she's been working with. Maybe that'll help us find the guy."

EIGHTEEN
Safe at Home?

Keep giving all the love you can…stand by
your man.
—*Stand By Your Man*, Tammy Wynette

"Jeff, thank god! You're OK?"

Casey was happy to see me and a bit enthusiastic in her greeting, meeting us in the driveway and hugging me tightly. My bruised ribs groaned in protest, but I realized I was feeling pretty relieved myself.

"Casey, this is Joe Landis, Jessie's brother."

"Oh, hi. I was really sorry to hear about your sister."

"Thanks. Listen, Brad, if I find anything I'll call you."

"Sure Joe, I'll stay in touch. And if there's anything I can do…"

He smiled just a little. "You folks have a great weekend, huh?"

As he drove away Casey gripped my arm.

"How much trouble are you really in, Jeff?" She asked, frightened.

I kissed her forehead. "It'll be OK," I said, as if I believed it. "Why don't we go on inside."

"Where are the girls?" I asked as we entered the house.

"They're napping."

"Voluntarily?" Casey and her youngest always had knock down drag outs over naptime. Cindy, the oldest, had just got to the point that she could stay up. It was particularly rare on the weekend, when the rules were a little more relaxed.

"All on their own. Cindy took Steph and they were both angels. Jeff…"

She had that warning tone in her voice. She wanted to know what happened.

"You're not hurt?"

"No, they just needed to ask a few questions."

"Who were those guys... and don't even think of telling me they were cops because they weren't!"

I hesitated.

"This is real trouble, isn't it? Those guys are the Mob."

My jaw dropped. "How could you know that?"

"The big guy who picked you up a few hours ago before, I had seen him before. He sometimes drives for Bobby."

"Bobby?"

You know Suzie next door, who watches the girls when we go out? Her boyfriend Bobby comes here in those black cars just like the one that got you or limos like the one that brought you back. Seriously, Jeff, how much trouble are we in?"

"Hey, I got an upgrade on the ride back, there's nothing to worry about." I wasn't reassured by that either. "The gospel truth is Case... I just plain don't know."

I sank a bit under my own sense of gravity.

"Jessie was part of the 'family.' I think I convinced them that I had nothing to do with what happened to her, for now, but who knows how, or when, they might change their minds."

"Then we're in serious trouble."

"We?"

"They found you *here*, Jeff." She said with a little distress in her voice.

That hadn't occurred to me. Not only had I managed to stick my own head into the bear trap, but I managed to involve Casey and the girls.

I had to start by keeping them safe. "Is there someplace you and the girls can go for a few days?"

"For how long, Jeff? It isn't like we could hide out forever. I mean, I know I'm worrying, but are we in real danger?"

"Hell, I don't even know if *I'm* in real danger. I just need to make sure you guys are safe."

"They want the killer, right? Not you. So what we have to do is just make sure they find him."

Who am I, Sherlock Holmes? How was I going to track down a killer? But I was already asking questions and curious. I had Mac and his police contacts, Joe was probably willing to help, and I could count on Casey for encouragement and a woman's perspective. After all, nobody had more reason to find the killer than I did.

I filled Casey in on the conversations I had had that afternoon.

"Well, at least they were friendlier than your drug dealing friends."

"Wouldn't take much," I said, reminded of the pain in my ribs, "With these guys I think any damage is apt to be more permanent."

She nodded. "So you're now skeptical about her being murdered over a drug deal. You think she was killed by a jealous boyfriend, instead?"

"I don't think they would have to be mutually exclusive. She wasn't a druggie, so if she was in the drug business it had to be either for the money, or for a guy. She never came across as greedy, but she always wanted..."

I trailed off, not really wanting to discuss Jessie's sexual proclivities with Casey. But she honed right in on it.

"Jeff, this is going to sound like a silly question in some ways, but what do you actually know about this girl? I mean I know you had a... you know..."

"We went out a few times, that's about it. She was mostly with Charlie and I spent most of my time with her friend, Linda."

"I don't mean to be nosy, but you were sleeping with her, Jessie, too, weren't you..."

"Well..."

"Do you think her brother was right when he implied she slept with every man she knew?"

"Wouldn't be surprised. It seemed to be something she always wanted to do."

Casey nodded. "Was it an obsession?"

I shrugged. Who doesn't want all they can get?

"Maybe she used the sex as a way of controlling her relationships? I know some women relate to men best on a sexual basis, maybe she uses it to escape dealing with men in ways she found uncomfortable."

"You mean, a guy can't ask her a lot of questions while he's 'on the job', right?"

"Exactly, using the intimacy of sex to avoid the intimacy of conversation, the question of genuine feeling..."

I nodded. "She might also really love an audience. I mean I told you about the shower thing."

"But that's not exactly an audience."

"Actually it is exactly an audience… from the Latin *audio*… but the thrill for her might not be that people will see her, so much as know what she's doing."

"I can see that point."

We sat silently for a moment.

"You mentioned her brother Joe," She started.

"Yeah?"

"You said she was telling him about her exploits… In some ways she was using sex to control her relationship with him, too."

"Not only that," I realized, "but evidence indicates she never had any great respect for the usual social boundaries. Could she have tried to seduce him?"

Casey nodded. "Subconsciously, at least. You might want to keep that in mind. Joe seems like a nice guy, but we all have our breaking point."

When I got back to Windsor, about 9 pm, Sunday, Ben, the desk clerk greeted me.

"Must have been quite a party."

I froze. "Party?" I asked.

His eyes narrowed. "I wasn't complaining, Brad, I was just kidding you."

"No, we haven't had a party lately. Mac's out of town and I've been over the river all weekend."

"Maybe one of your friends?"

"No, not that I know of."

"Had to be something, the girls were complaining that the place was… well, a bit messy. Usually there's a little extra for them if there's extra work. Maybe they were just grumbling."

Maybe. On the other hand, there were at least two crime rings that thought I had or knew something useful to them. It wouldn't be tough for them to find somebody to ransack the apartment.

It's a cold chill down the spine. Home is the one place where you always want to feel safe, but knowing that dangerous people can get to you was hardly going to make sleep easier to come by that night.

"Thanks, Ben, we'll try to be more careful in the future."

NINETEEN
Cops and crooks

(Jingle) C—K—L—W... The Motor City.
It's One o'clock at the big 8 on a gorgeous Monday afternoon,
Big Bill Davis checking In with Booker T & The M Gs, don't
you love those 'Green Onions', (song-instrumental).

"Hey, Brad, you remember Nancy, the girl from
Chucklehead's party? She invited me to go with her over to the
Rooster Tail tonight. Marvin Gaye and Tammy Terrell are doing
this week's Motown Night. Why don't you get a girl and come
with us."

I shook my head.

"Hey, you had a rough weekend, buddy. Maybe a little fun
tonight can get your week back on track."

"Yeah, I don't know..."

"Look it's a shame about that Jessie girl, but you can't just
sit around feeling sorry for yourself."

I understood that much, but I don't think I was up to
anything too involved after my frenetic weekend. I could use a
quiet evening at home.

Then again...

"Sure, why not?"

I tried Linda, not really expecting she'd want to go, but
surprisingly, she agreed without hesitating. I drove over with
Mac while the girls came their own way. We both figured to
spend the night on the US side.

The Rooster Tail was a restaurant on the river near the site of
the annual Gold Cup Hydroplane race, the name coming from
the plume of water thrown up by the propellers of the racing
boats. The building was a two-decker that sat on the water, with
a boat dock to collect patrons from the various Detroit yacht
clubs.

Nancy met us in the parking lot when we arrived, but I was surprised to also find the Detroit cop, Talbert, tapping my shoulder as we got to the doorway.

"Well, Sgt. Talbert, are we going to pretend that this meeting is a coincidence?"

He didn't rise to the bait on that.

"I see you're in strict mourning eh, Tommy? You don't mind me calling you Tommy... or is it Tom, Chandler?"

"Actually all my friends and family call me Jeff."

"Jesus Christ!" he grumbled. "How many names does any one person need?"

I smiled at him, but didn't take the bait either.

"What can I do for you, Sgt. Talbert?"

"I think you know something you're not telling me. Something that could help solve this case."

He might have been right, I suppose, but it didn't seem useful to agree with him.

"Like?" I prompted.

"I think you know who was smuggling drugs with the Royce woman."

"Actually, you're wrong, I'm not entirely convinced she was smuggling drugs."

His eyebrows shot upward.

"What are you saying? Do you know some other reason why somebody wanted to kill her?"

There were certainly enough people interested in Jessie to suggest other possibilities, but I didn't have any specifics.

"No, can't say that I do."

"What about her girlfriend, the Stevenson girl? Could she be involved?"

I suddenly recognized the reason for Talbert's presence at the restaurant that night. He was shadowing Linda. Then, when he saw me show up, he decided to try me again. Now, of course, the two of us will probably be seen by him as co-conspirators.

"Don't you have to establish there's something to be involved with first? Look, I don't know anything you don't know, Sgt. Talbert. If I discover anything I'll let you know... good enough?"

"NO! Not good enough... *Jeff.* To be honest, I think you're lying! You and this Stevenson girl are in this up to your necks. I'll bet you're meeting her here tonight."

That confirmed the assumption he was tailing Linda.

"To be honest, *Joe*," I matched his sarcastic tone, "my social life is of no concern to you. As for my being 'involved', wouldn't there have to be something for me to be 'involved in'?"

"Oh, don't worry wise guy, we'll find out what you're involved in."

"When you do, would you let me know? As I said before, I've got nothing to hide."

He continued to glare suspiciously at me.

"I can go in, right?"

"Yeah, yeah." He mumbled. "Just remember *Brad*... I'll be watching."

I found the rest of the gang at a table on the top deck of the restaurant.

"Who was that?" Mac asked.

"A Detroit cop named Talbert. He's investigating the murder. We're under suspicion."

"Mac's a suspect?" Nancy asked excitedly.

I was a little worried until I saw the twinkle in her eye.

"No. Linda and I," I confirmed.

"What? She was my best friend!" Linda squawked. "Why would I kill her?"

"I don't know that he thinks one of us killed her so much as we know why she was killed. He followed you here."

"Followed me?"

"I'm pretty sure. He probably thinks Jessie told you something."

"She wasn't dealing drugs! She needed the... oh, who cares? She was never in the drug business. You knew her, Brad. Didn't it have to be something else?"

I didn't know Jessie for certain, but I was having trouble seeing her as some kind of drug kingpin like our friend Charlton. But the one possibility was that Jessie might have been living beyond her means to keep up with Linda. Linda might have kept her friend's more humble income in mind, but Jessie might have become competitive and sought drugs as a source of fast money.

"I'm sure somebody will find the answers, Linda."

I just hoped the answers weren't us.

"...Ain't no mountain high enough, ain't no valley low enough, ain't no river wide enough to keep me from getting to you..."

As the concert continued, a tall black man dressed entirely in black was heading toward our table. Turtleneck, coat, pants... well, he was wearing white shoes. It took me a few seconds to place him.

He smiled broadly as he passed with a nod.

"Good to see you, Mr. Walker," he said politely.

"John," I acknowledged.

I could feel my ribs ache again, but refused to look around for Charlton or the rest of the gang.

"Friend of yours?" Linda asked.

"No. Just a fellow I met at a recording studio."

"He's very handsome," Nancy said.

As the concert ended, Mac and Nancy left, while Linda and I stayed to have another drink.

"What should I do, Brad?" She asked, earnestly. "About the police following me?"

"Don't run red lights," I said with a grin.

"No! How do I get rid of them?"

"I'm not sure you can, why would you want to?"

"It's embarrassing... humiliating. It's frightening having somebody watching you all the time, keeping track of everything you do and everyone you meet..."

"But if you've got nothing to hide I suppose..."

I stopped. I had no point.

"What do you mean IF I've got nothing to hide?"

"Hold it. I didn't mean it like that and I'm realizing you're right anyway. I think you have a right to complain to the police if you feel you're being harassed by them. You're a law-abiding citizen who is willing to answer any questions. They should have to give you a reason for following you."

"You're saying they'll stop following me if I complain?"

"Probably not, but they might have to justify it to their bosses which could get them to change their tactics. Then again, your dad is a prominent businessman, so maybe complaining could stop them."

On the way out of the club, Matt Donovan literally bumped into me.

"Oh, sorry... Hey, Brad, how are you?"

"I'm OK."

Hey, listen, I've got my boat here. We're going to do a little midnight cruise on the river. Maybe you and your friend might want to join us?"

It was sort of tempting. I generally liked boating, but I still really couldn't comfortably face the river.

"Thanks," I said, "but no."

"Oh, come on."

"I have to be on the air in the morning." I said, grasping for a reasonable excuse.

He shrugged. "Maybe some other time."

"Sure, some other time."

He headed off toward the docks.

Linda watched him leave, brow furrowed.

"You know, he looks kind of familiar…"

Familiar? Did Jessie know Donovan, was Linda part of the 'family' as well.

"What?" I tried to sound calm. "What do you mean familiar?"

"You know… he looks like that TV actor! The one from that detective show…"

I shook my head. "Can't say I know who you mean."

TWENTY
Understanding the Game

Love is just like a baseball game… three
strikes you're out.
         (Love is Like a) Baseball Game,
                     —The Intruders

Mac and I were cruising across the Ambassador Bridge, enjoying another 'top down' day.

"A Tigers game?" I asked him.

Yeah," Mac said. "My guy at the FBI does undercover work and tries to avoid the office whenever possible. I think he also enjoys setting up these little anonymous meetings. He always wanted to be James Bond."

I smiled a little. I wasn't the world's greatest baseball fan, but sitting out in the sun at the stadium drinking beer and watching baseball wasn't the worst plan for a late spring day.

We arrived during the first inning. Our seats were down the first base side just at the beginning of the bullpen area, about twelve rows from the field on the aisle. The third seat was occupied by a tall sort of balding man in his 30's, dark hair, and one of those non-descript faces.

"Brad Walker, Carl Marchek," Mac introduced.

"Hi." I said, offering a hand.

He gestured out toward the field.

"You ever wonder how he does that?"

I frowned in confusion.

"McAuliffe, the way he corkscrews that bat way up over his head. How does he ever manage to get around on a pitch, especially a major league fastball?"

I watched the Tiger second baseman foul a ball into the stands behind third base.

"Don't ask me," I said. "I never could hit worth a damn. Maybe he realized he had been swinging too early and just decided to slow his swing down a bit."

We sat through the end of the inning in silence. Then he fixed me with a piercing glance, then gave a big smile. "You want to know about the drug trade in Detroit, why?"

"A friend of mine was killed. Cops think she was involved in the drug trade…"

"You weren't involved were you? Because if you're in trouble, I can put you in touch with someone at the US attorney's office who can…"

"No, I wasn't involved."

"Why get involved now?"

Because I found out I was suspect number 1?

"Well, it's sort of personal. I think another friend might also be in trouble, so I hope I can find a way to help her… him… without involving any cops—no offense."

"None taken. Oh, crap!"

Baltimore's Frank Robinson drilled a line drive over the right field wall. Al Kaline, playing right field, barely bothered to look up.

"He hit that a ton," Mac said, several neighboring fans turned to look at him, thinking he was a radio broadcast, I think.

"Shake it off, Denny," Marchek shouted toward the mound.

"OK, hypothetically, let's just say your dead friend is the girl they found in the river the other day. What drug was she involved with?"

I guess it didn't take Sherlock Holmes to know who the friend might be, and I knew Mac had assured me that he would keep the whole thing unofficial, but…

"Don't worry, this is all hypothetical, like I told McCarthy. An excuse to get out of the office and see a ballgame."

"She might have been running cocaine."

"That would put her in competition with our old friend, Bobby Charlton. As far as we know, he's the main pipeline across the river. Do you know who was on the receiving end?"

I shrugged. "No idea."

"Do you know who was supplying her with the drug?"

"Got me."

He scratched his chin for a moment. I knew what he was thinking. He was thinking—'how can I help a guy who doesn't know anything?' He stared out at the field for a few moments.

"She have any ties with bikers?"

Bikers? "Not that I know, but we'd only known each other a short time."

"Does your other friend?"

"Probably not. Why bikers?"

"Look, she had to have a pipeline to get the coke." He turned toward me. "The coke comes in from down south by plane or boat, mostly on the Gulf coast. Organized major operators like Charlton move the stuff by phony shipments to legitimate companies, long haul truckers, and several other dodges.

"There are also individuals and 'Mom and Pop' operations that might supply a one time deal, but aren't very good for a consistent network.

"So the most likely pipeline would be your biker gangs. For a percentage of the haul, bikers would have no qualms about the morality of the deal, they travel everywhere, won't rat each other out and are used to ducking the police.

"Why couldn't it be, as you put it, a one shot deal?"

"It could be, but then why kill her? She would have to be challenging Charlton's set up in some way for him to bother wouldn't she? A big mover like Charlton wouldn't sweat a one shot deal. While we're on the subject, I just don't see how you or your friend could be in any danger if you're not involved. Her pipeline guys might find a way to approach you, but I don't see how they can drag you into this, nor why they'd trust you in the first place."

I decided not to tell him that I had met Charlton and he was definitely sweating this deal… even with Jessie dead. But he was also right about it not making sense.

"Could it be the Mob?" I asked, trying to be casual.

"C'mon, Norm," he shouted at the Tiger first baseman who had swung mightily and missed. "Nah, they have been adamant about not handling any drugs. They have, however, sometimes provided logistical and financial support for big operators like Charlton."

"So Charlton is the most likely to have killed her?"

"Maybe, but it just seems so unlike his usual style. Besides, why just this girl, could she have been the brains behind the thing?"

I thought for a second. Jessie was nobody's fool, but "Not a chance."

"Are you certain it wasn't heroin she was moving, hypothetically?"

"Don't think so, why?"

"Heroin would put her into the hands of Mitchell Martin. Now Martin might be your killer 'cause he's just insane. He would kill a girl over a kilo or two. We're going to need a beer for this story."

We flagged a vendor and fetched a couple of beers.

"OK, Mitch Martin was a Detroit cop who they fired for brutality and corruption—apparently he was pathological about both. He had already been dealing various drugs while on duty, so he used his connections and friendships with cops and ex-cops to eliminate the competition and work his way to the top of the heroin trade.

"Unlike the other movers in the drug business, the syndicate will provide him with no help at all. The old animosities keep them from any kind of cooperation. But there are unfortunately enough crooked cops in Detroit to supply Mitch with all the help he needs."

He took a long pull of his beer, "He has a particularly nasty habit of lopping off fingers, one joint at a time, until he gets what he wants. The joke is: you can always tell Mitch's friends because they all still have *nine* fingers."

"You mean ten," Mac said.

"No," I said. "Even his friends are bound to disagree with him."

Mac grimaced.

"He'd be the choice for killing the girl, but he would never be on the river in a boat. He can't swim and is scared to death of water. Won't even drink his scotch on the rocks.

"The closest he comes to the water is season tickets for the Red Wings."

That got a laugh out of me.

"There you go, Gator!" he shouted, as Gates Brown looped a double into left-center to even the score at 2 each. Baltimore pitcher Dave McNally kicked at the dirt in front of the pitching rubber, muttering angrily to himself.

"Of course, he could have gotten any of his nine fingered henchmen to dump her in the river after he strangled her… but then again, he would have wanted to make sure who else she was working with and…"

"All Jessie's fingers were accounted for." It was a slip, but he knew anyway. *Did he know Linda, too?*

He smiled. "But only one foot."

I don't know if I reacted or if he just expected one, but he turned to say something to me, when the crack of the bat brought his attention back onto the field. Catcher Bill Freehan had stroked a solid single to center, with Brown scampering home to take a 3-2 lead.

"My brother went to U of M with him," he said, indicating Freehan at first base. "All around good guy, not just on the baseball diamond."

"What about smugglers on the Windsor side?"

"One stop shopping. Fellow named Cristafaro Ferante. Handsome little fellow, one of those Ronald Coleman mustaches. Owns a legitimate import-export outfit. Hasn't been on this side, but just like the others, could have hired it out, but again why? There had to be somebody on *that* side, he'd probably go after them, not her."

"Any other possible drugs?"

He shook his head. "The rest is just batshit, pardon the expression. Pot is everywhere, everyone and their cousin in both directions. LSD, the idiots cook up in their basements, chemicals available on either side. Girl wasn't a chemist, was she?"

"Don't think so."

"Look, it could be almost anybody, but it wouldn't be a player we know yet. I think it's a lot more likely she was double crossed by her own confederates."

Well, that narrows it down.

"Afraid I'm not helping much."

"I guess I didn't give you much to work with."

"Well it did get me out of the office and into the ball park. Seriously, whoever killed that girl is dangerous, I'd be happy to help you get him, hypothetically." He said chuckling.

Frank Robinson, one of the most feared hitters in baseball, hit a smoker that Denny McLain caught in self-defense.

"That McLain is a lucky son of a bitch," Marchek said. "With his luck he's gonna end up winning 30 games."

TWENTY—ONE
The Condemned Man's Last Meal

More Music... C-K-L-W
It's 7:28 on a Tuesday evening, Tim Sheldon at the Big 8 with
music by Jim Morrison and the Doors...
Vocal: *Hello, I love you, won't you tell me your name...*

When I got home from the ballpark, I found two notes at the
front desk. The first was from our star evening DJ, Tim
Sheldon, thanking us for the use of the apartment. Tim had a
pair of local women and, rumor had it, at least one young man
who he kept company with. We occasionally let him make use
of our apartment for his extracurriculars.

The second message was a bit more ominous:

> *Please join me and my associates for dinner this evening at*
> *Ye Olde Steak House. About 7:30.*
>
> C. Ferante

Ferante was the fellow Marchek described as the Windsor
end of the drug smuggling trade, so it was no stretch to assume
his polite invitation included an unwritten post script of *or else*.

I was beginning to become tired of being dragged in and
questioned by a rogue's gallery of evil characters without having
any reasonable answers. I hoped the public location of this
meeting would at least spare me another beating.

Ye Olde Steak House sat on Goyeau Street near the tunnel
entrance. It was a one story wood building with the stucco and
timber façade of a Swiss farmhouse. As I walked in, I
recognized Ferante immediately from Carl Marchek's
description, but tried to show no sign of it. Although he had the
moustache that gave him the general look of a famed Hollywood
star, he wasn't really much to look at, an effeminate little guy
with a fat, doughy sort of face.

The other man at the table faced the world with a vicious scowl. An angry, violent sort of man. With no reason or evidence, I decided that he could only be Mitchell Martin, a man willing to cut off your fingers if he didn't like your answers.

I introduced myself to the *maitre'd* who conducted me to the table.

"Good evening, Mr. Walker. We're pleased you could join us this evening." He indicated the seat before him with a gesture. "What can we get you to drink?"

"Oh," I was a bit startled. "Uh, just a beer."

"Of course, a draft beer for our friend, Fritz." The waiter left. "I've heard your radio program, Mr. Walker. My daughter tells me it's the most popular station in town."

I smiled. I usually would answer that by saying something about how even though we were on top across the river in Detroit and other cities, we weren't number one in Windsor yet, but it died on the way to my mouth. Martin was staring at me, or was he just looking at my hands?

"So then, Mr. Walker," he said, misreading my expression, or maybe reading my sub conscious. "You want to know why we invited you to meet with us. We'll all enjoy our dinner more if we take a moment to get nasty business out of the way."

I'll admit to being a bit disconcerted by the combination of Martin's malicious scowl and Ferante's choice of words, but I was hoping he meant that phrase in the sense of 'I hate business' nasty, not that the business was about to turn nasty.

"I was sorry to hear that a mutual friend of ours seems to have died tragically some days ago."

Ferante was clearly a man who loved his euphemism.

"Thanks," I said. "She was clearly pretty popular."

"I have no doubt that you have spoken to several of her friends and associates, and I suppose the police have also had questions."

"Listen, maybe I can save you several questions. Jessie didn't tell me anything about what she was doing. I don't know any of the people she associated with. She didn't leave anything with me, nor, as far as I know, with anyone else.

"In fact, since you were in business with her, maybe you can answer a few questions for me... What is it I'm supposed to have for you? Drugs? Money? Something else?"

Martin's scowl cracked into something resembling a vicious smile. Ferante scowled angrily. I recognized that I had violated the rules of euphemism. I needed to be more careful.

"I'm sorry, the police used that word and I was following their assumption. My concern here is that I have no idea what Jessie... excuse me, our friend, is supposed have left behind. Let's start again.

"I understand you're in the business of import and export. Let's say, hypothetically, (thanks, Carl Marchek) there are times when you wouldn't want to trouble the overworked folks at the Customs bureau. Our mutual friend was supposedly helping you to move some..." I thought back to a business course I took at the University of Toledo, "widgets across the border."

"Widgets?" Martin chuckled. Ferante smiled a bit.

"Just in case," he said, "your assumption is correct, What do you want to know?"

"Our mutual friend was involved in an operation and something went wrong. What sort of packet did she get away with?"

"Why should we tell you anything?" Martin challenged.

"Well, if I'm involved I should already know some of the details, if I don't, I can't really know where to start looking for it. And a lot of people seem to think I'm the only one who has any chance of finding it."

"I think you already got our widgets," Martin growled.

"Well, somebody already searched my apartment," I answered. "Hey, if I was planning to double-cross you, why would I ask questions?"

"This is all interesting, but why would you help us find what we want, even in theory?" Ferante asked.

Why?

—Because Jessie might just have played me for a sucker, and I had to wonder if it wasn't deliberate?

—Because all of these gangsters weren't going to give me a moment's peace until I found what they were looking for or they were pointed elsewhere?

"Because," I said, "maybe what happened to the stuff might help us find out who killed the girl."

Ferante nodded slowly. "A noble motive, but how do we guarantee the confidentiality of our discussions?"

"I don't need to know any vital facts that would concern the cops like who or where, just *how* the job went wrong."

"We can trust you?"

"As much as I can trust you. Maybe more. I'm on the air five days a week from 9 to noon."

It wasn't that I wasn't shaking, but I knew they could just be waiting to kill me anyway.

He laughed. "You are right, a foolish question." He turned to the booth behind him. "Michael, could you describe the probable transaction in question to Mr. Walker here."

He stood. "I have another meeting. My associate, Mr. Lang, will answer any additional questions you have. Please feel free to have what you would like for dinner. We have already taken care of your bill."

"Thank you," I answered, inclining my head.

"Just for the record," he added. "My friend Mr. Martin was not involved in this particular piece of business, but he felt he should have a look at you."

That sent a chill down my spine.

A gangly blond haired guy about my height (6' 2") stepped around from the booth behind me and sat down.

"Michael Lang." He introduced himself.

"Brad Walker."

"You need to understand, Walker. If you cross these people, you're going to end up very, very, dead."

TWENTY–TWO
Jessie's Secrets

You're dynamite, you got me uptight... the way
you sock it to me girl, you're outa sight
                    —*Heartbreaker*, Gene Pitney

"You know, Walker," Mac joked, "At this rate you're going to become the next Al Capone."

"Fuck you," I grumbled. "And the horse you rode in on."

It wasn't funny. I had at least three people who were willing to kill me if I couldn't do what they wanted. Worse, even if I could please one of them, the result would most likely infuriate the others.

"Hey, Brad, just kidding..."

I shrugged. "Yeah, I know. Thanks."

"I did get one piece of news from my guy at Detroit Police. Jessie's husband, Matt Royce, is listed as missing."

"Missing in action?"

"Not exactly. He's what they call AWOL, absent without leave. He was wounded on the battlefield and was recuperating in a Saigon hospital. He had a head injury and leg wound and they were supposed to be shipping him back to the States for further recovery when he pulled a disappearing act somewhere between here and there."

"OK, Tell me how you lose a wounded man?"

"Well, he was ambulatory, so they must have just given him a ticket and sent him to the airport."

"So, how do they know he's not still over there?"

"They don't, really. What the Army told the police was that someone flew to the States under his name, but he has since disappeared, and they are certain that the 'Royce' who flew back was not Jessie's husband."

"Meaning he was black?"

"That was my guy's assumption." Mac thought for a second, "I just had a weird thought, what if he's here?"

"Isn't that the Army's assumption?" I asked.

"No, I mean *here*, on this side, in Canada"

It was my turn to look puzzled.

"Sure," Mac continued. "With all these draft dodgers and the like up here, he'd just be another American expatriate."

It actually did make some sense, and it would explain why Jessie didn't want to admit she was spending time on this side of the border, or even that she knew her way around.

"In fact," I speculated, "maybe she got involved in the drug business trying to raise a nest egg for them."

"Do you think we can find him?"

"I don't think so. The army has a lot more resources than we do. We don't have much of a chance."

"Unless he's here in Canada."

"Unless, of course, he's here."

"So, Sherlock, did your latest conversation with the leaders of the underworld give you any useful clues to this caper?"

"This guy is clearly not as full of threats or as inclined to casual violence as our other drug lords, and certainly not psychotic like Mitchell Martin, who I also met tonight, but I think he would be much more dangerous. His style is much more sophisticated. First time, he might have a quiet chat, but his next step would be to kill you—or as he would say 'arrange a tragic unpleasant demise.'"

I paused for a second.

"On the other hand he's the first one confident enough to sort of fill me in on the details of what Jessie was doing the night of her little misadventure. So when he has me killed, I'll at least have some vague idea why."

"Decent of him."

"According to Ferante's right hand man, Michael Lang, Jessie represented their link to a new outfit smuggling coke across the border. They were doing a small deal as a test, when it was raided by somebody. She slipped off into the darkness with the drugs, they think. They figured the delivery outfit guys probably got the cash, but they aren't certain, because Jessie was their contact for those guys.

"Ferante's people think Charlton was behind the raid—they were, after all, working his side of the street."

"Any idea how much dope, how much money?"

I shook my head. "I suggested they shouldn't give me too many details about these things because the less you know, the less they can kill you over."

"You think that will work?"

"Probably not, but why make sure you know too much. Besides, I have to hope your friend Marchek is right that really big operators don't really sweat over a single transaction."

"Especially since the girl is dead and she's the only one who knew all the players."

"Exactly,"

"Did you at least get dinner?"

"I had the surf and turf. I figured if those guys were our killers, it might be my last decent meal, so I tried to make the most of it."

TWENTY–THREE
Mustang Sally

Mustang Sally… think you better slow that
Mustang down…
                    -*Mustang Sally*, Wilson Pickett

After the show Wednesday, I drove the Corvette down to the fort at Amherstburg, just to add some miles for the contest. I called in, came back, hit the liquor store, then went home. I was listening to Stevie Wonder when I got a call.

"Hey Brad, It's Joe Landis."

"Hey Joe, How are you?"

"OK, I guess. Just called for two things. One, Jess's funeral is going to be Thursday morning in Dearborn. I thought it was better to bury her with Papa and Ma out in Clinton."

"Everybody else OK with that?"

"Yeah. Dino actually encouraged it. He's going to arrange for Mom to come, and will stay away so she doesn't get upset."

"OK, I'll be there."

The phone went silent.

"Joe? You said there were two things?"

"Yeah… I'm not sure what it means exactly, but I called Jess's Kelly agency, just pretending to be curious about her last check.

"She hadn't been there for six months!"

"Which raises the question: Where has she been working?" I wondered.

"Or even if… You don't suppose that was why she was…"

"Not necessarily. It probably means she found a job elsewhere."

I suppose it was possible she had just decided to make a living doing what she seemed to want to do most of the time, but I couldn't help thinking about what Casey had said about her using sex as a way to control her relationships and not just seek satisfaction. Random encounters with strangers seemed to run contrary to that philosophy.

"Call the Kelly people back. See if they will tell you the last place she worked. Sometimes people hire the girls directly."

I thought I should check with Linda and see if she expected us to go together to the funeral. It also occurred to me that she would know where Jessie was working. She might tell me even if she wouldn't tell Joe.

"Hey, Linda."

"Hi, Brad."

"I didn't know if you heard... Jessie's funeral is set for Thursday."

"I heard, Joe called me. Could we go together? I'd appreciate a strong arm to cling to."

"Sure, if you want."

"Thanks, Brad."

"No problem. Joe asked me an interesting question."

"Really?"

"He wanted to know where she'd been working. As you know, she hadn't worked at Kelly for about six months. I was wondering if you knew where she went."

Silence.

"No idea," she finally said. I could hear my bullshit alarm clanging. I waited.

"Look, I knew she left Kelly, but she didn't want Joe to know... apparently he used to check up on her. Anyways, I know at the end of last year, she was working at... of all things a radio station, after that I have no idea."

I didn't believe her, but I figured there was no advantage in calling her a liar, any more than challenging Jessie that night. But why didn't she say something, leave a message in the two or three days before somebody killed her. I had checked at the desk for a message, but... maybe that was too obvious. She needed to send me a message that only I might look for.

"Hey, Linda, has anybody asked you about Jessie's car?"

"The Mustang? Yeah, the cops asked if I knew where it was. But nobody's found it yet"

"Any general idea where it might be?"

"I thought you decided it was on your side of the river?"

"An assumption only because I don't know how she got over here that night."

"If you're right and somebody tried to kill her when she came to see you, she had to know she was exposing you to danger, right? So she couldn't have left you a message someplace obvious—where somebody else could intercept it—it had to be something only you would know. Did you guys have a special place?"

"Special place? With the exception of that night, everyplace I saw her I was with you."

"Listen, Brad, you don't have to worry about my feelings. I had become used to sharing my men with Jessie."

It was clear from her tone, she was trying to convince herself as much as me. I had always sort of assumed that the two girls were similar in attitudes about men, but maybe they weren't. Perhaps Linda's sexual adventurousness wasn't about enjoying the experience, but an attempt to compete with Jessie.

"Jessie and I never soloed, darlin'. Honest to God."

She was silent for a moment.

"Well whatever it is… it would have to be something personal. You sure she never left a note at the desk?"

"I'm sure."

"You know, I might have mentioned your real name to her. Would they have still recognized you at the Front Desk?"

"Yeah, my given name is on the lease. Even if somebody was new and didn't know, one of the others would have noticed and recognized me."

Then it occurred to me. The most obvious and secure way to deliver a note. And it only took four cents.

TWENTY—FOUR
Shadows in the dark

I walked down to the front desk and found Patrick, the fellow who was at the desk when Jessie came in.

"Hey, Patrick, I was wondering about the girl who came to see me a few weeks ago."

"Sure. I heard she was the one who was killed over in Detroit, I'm sorry," he said. "I think I know what you're thinking, but the police questioned all of us and we double checked. She didn't return to leave any packages or envelopes for you or for anyone else."

"Did she make any phone calls?"

"No, of course not, I would have remembered something like that. She did post a letter, if that means anything."

"She posted it that night she came in, distressed?"

"Yes, she asked for an envelope and bought a stamp."

"Did you see who it was addressed to?"

He grinned at me. "Handling the post is a sacred responsibility. I would never read anyone's mail... besides I couldn't see it. She filled it in at that desk and dropped it in the box over there."

He pointed to a mailbox built into the wall.

"I can tell you she only bought a 4 center, so it was probably somewhere here in Windsor."

"Why didn't you mention this sooner?"

"I don't know. I figured whoever got the letter would tell the cops if it was significant."

He would have been right, but I hadn't got the letter, yet. But I certainly would tomorrow.

Built originally as the Customs House, the main Windsor Post Office was an imposing edifice at the corner of Oulette Avenue and Pitt Street.

I found a humorless, middle-aged clerk, the type all post offices seem to mass produce.

"My name is Chandler, Jeff Chandler; I think there's a letter for me in General Delivery."

"Just a minute." The clerk returned, handing me a Holiday Inn envelope. In it were two Ford keys wrapped in a piece of Holiday Inn stationery.

Now I just had to find the car that they fit.

I decided to wait until after dark, so I didn't have to worry as much about somebody recognizing me while I was searching around Windsor for the car.

I would have found the car on day one if I knew it had been left for me to find. It was in the Holiday Inn parking lot, down along the river. I thought I should check out the car before reporting it to the cops, in case... no, I was just plain curious. I really had no idea what to expect, but it seemed a bad idea to give the police anything that they might use to cause trouble for me or my friends. There also had to be something she left for one of us. Might as well have a look first.

I put on my driving gloves—no need confusing the cops with extra fingerprints—and opened the passenger–side door. Nothing much in the glove box except the owner's manual, a pair of stockings, a packet of tissues and several unused condoms. I was a bit surprised, knowing that Jessie was pretty quick to mention she was on the pill, but better safe than sorry, I guess.

A small flask was tucked under the passenger side seat and an umbrella was stashed under the driver's side. There was nothing else of note.

X marks the spot was in the trunk. Under a casually tossed quilt, that would only have kept it out of clear view, was a TWA flight bag that had to be holding what they all were looking for. I just undid the zipper and dropped the hip flask into it then carried it up to the apartment.

I decided to stash the stuff in my room, so Mac could have some claim that he didn't know if anyone searched the place.

The flight bag held five plastic wrapped foil covered blocks—each a kilo, I assumed. It was the only place the metric system ever took hold in the States, I mused. I didn't have a clue to what the exact value of the stuff might be, but it was probably worth killing for. The question was: *What should I do with it?*

If I just handed it to the cops, we wouldn't learn anything new, would we? Plus, if it came down to Talbert, he'd have me locked up for both the drugs and Jessie's murder. I didn't fancy giving it to Charlton or Ferante, because it would end up on the street. Destroying it had some appeal, but I also thought it just might come in handy as bait for the killer.

I decided to stash it and think. But where?

As I surveyed the closet, I decided to hide the dope in my, mostly unused, golf bag. My uncle had given me a set of his old clubs in case I took up the game, but I had had little interest except for one girl who belonged to a country club near Ft. Wayne.

I tried to be careful in placing the bricks at the bottom of the bag and returning the clubs, figuring the dust accumulation on the club heads would be discouragement to any would be searchers.

I sat for a moment wondering if Jessie had been killed over the "widgets" I just stashed. Suddenly the room seemed cold. I decided I needed to move, so I went off to have a couple of beers around town, someplace, anyplace where there were people.

It was on the way back from Sid's at the end of the night, that I felt something unusual. I wasn't really sure what it was, but I could feel a chill crawl down my back. That thing you tend to get when you drop a glass in a restaurant or do something else that draws everyone's eyes to you. I stopped and looked back. I didn't see anyone, but that sort of uneasy feeling was still with me.

Just as I got to the entrance of the Holiday Inn, I took another look over my shoulder, and saw something moving in the shadows across the street. I kept looking back for a second... I wanted my shadow to move again or something. Was someone following me, or was I just getting jumpy?

Who would be following me? I don't think Talbert could get away with following me in Canada, and I wouldn't think the Canadian cops were really that interested. I must have been imagining things.

How long had he been following me? Did he know that I had found Jessie's car? Did he see me with the dope? Maybe the best move would be to just call the RCMP and have them take charge of the dope—of course, now that I had the stuff in my apartment, I wondered if they would believe I just 'found it'.

It was another one of those moments when I found myself thinking not only that I was in over my head, but that I had no chance of getting myself back out of this thing.

TWENTY-FIVE
Jessie's Funeral

*It's Nine o'clock at the Big 8, with Steve Williams filling in
for Brad Walker... man, I sure hope you weren't taking the
day off to play golf...*

I was on my way to pick up Linda for Jessie's funeral when I
heard Steve signing on, and had to chuckle. It wasn't just golf, it
was surely a lousy day to do *anything* outdoors. The rain had
been falling steadily since last night, and showed no sign of
letting up. It was rainy, one of those ugly, humid days where the
rain never puts a dent in the temperature, but just makes the day
more unbearable. I promised myself I was getting air
conditioning in my next car, no more convertibles.

I pulled into the driveway on Beacon Hill Rd, and Linda
came skittering across the pavement in her high heels, carrying a
pretty blue umbrella (she obviously loved blue stuff). She backed
into the car and shook off the umbrella as she leaned back across
the seat to kiss me and said, ironically: "Perfect weather for a
funeral isn't it?"

"If this is an early indication, it's gonna be a long, hot
summer," I grumbled, "my next car is gonna be air conditioned!"

"Hey, why don't we take Mom's car," Linda said, "it's air
conditioned."

"Fine idea," I said, pulling forward and stopping in front of
the garage door that contained Linda's car.

"Mom and Dad are out of town again, so she won't be
needing it," Linda said, as she jumped out, opening the blue
umbrella and clicking over to door number three. She stuck a

key in the lock and the door glided open revealing a gold Olds Toronado.

Hoo-ah, I thought, *that's what I want to get next.*

I jumped out and ran to join her in the enormous garage, which also contained a new black Buick Le Sabre, Linda's GTO convertible, and a 1961 Chevy Impala.

"That's the car I learned to drive in," Linda smiled, "and now Brandy is using it, under supervision of course. We just can't let a 16 year old run wild can we?"

We both chuckled at that one, remembering the pool party a while back.

A few minutes later we were gliding along, in Mrs. Stevenson's new Toronado, comfortably cool, and headed for Goldstein-O'Brien funeral home in Dearborn.

"First time I ever drove a front wheel drive," I said, "I like the way it handles."

"My dad loves to drive it too," Linda said, "I think he drives it more than Mom."

Looking in the rearview mirror, I noticed that a blue Ford was still behind us, as it had been for the past few minutes, since we left Linda's house.

"We have company," I said, "see the blue Ford back there? I'm pretty sure that's our cop, Sgt. Talbert!"

Even as the rain picked up toward a serious downpour, I noticed several bikers were seemingly following along behind the "unmarked" Ford. Only a man , or should I say MEN on a mission would be out cruising motorcycles in a downpour like this. One of the Harleys roared past the cop, and pulled in behind Linda and me. He was wearing a sleeveless leather vest, and a sopping wet blue bandana on his head. It was a wonder he could see at all, with the rain pounding his face, but he didn't seem fazed by it… perhaps because he rode his Harley, rain or shine, and was used to it. I always wondered how those guys got around in the winter, but didn't have time to think more about that, as he suddenly roared past the Toronado, and pulled in front of us. On the back of his vest were the words "Paladins M C", across the top, and "Toledo Ohio" at the bottom, with a chess piece in the middle, reminiscent of the business card offered by the hero in the old TV Western, *Have Gun Will Travel.*

I said to Linda, "Mr. Paladin there might have a gun, and is surely traveling, but what in the hell is he doing out here in this

weather?" She started to say something, but stopped as the other
bikers pulled around us from both sides to join formation with
their lead bike just ahead of us.

"Those fuckers are crazy," I growled, "pulling that kind of
shit in this weather."

"What the hell is going on!" Linda yelled over the bike roar,
"First that cop, now these clowns. Don't tell me there're after
us, too!"

"Let's just see where they go", I answered, "They're
probably just out to screw around with someone, and we are the
chosen screwees."

But even as I tried to reassure her, I was pretty sure she was
right, this was no random act, and add to that the fact that they
were from *Toledo*?

At that moment, the bikers pulled into the left lane like
fighter planes in formation, and sped off into the distance. At the
risk of repeating myself I muttered, "Those fuckers are crazy."

We pulled into the parking lot at Goldstein-O'Brien funeral
home at 9:55, with a few minutes to spare. I was right in my
original suspicion, Talbert *was* driving the Ford, and pulled in
right beside us.

I pushed the Toronado's center armrest up, and said to
Linda: "Slide over and get out on my side, let's avoid that
prick."

She handed me the umbrella and I opened the door, we both
slid out quickly and headed for the funeral parlor. I didn't notice
any Harleys parked nearby, but if they were there we'd see them
soon enough.

The smell is always the same. Every funeral home I've ever
been to has the identical fragrance of various types of flowers
colliding in the air, but under the surface, a disturbing vague
smell of death, or embalming chemicals, or something, that is
just a little disturbing. There was a white casket, closed, of
course, with a beautiful framed picture of Jessie on top. The
group of people was rather small, mostly family, and some of
Jessie's friends, I supposed, none of which I knew. Linda didn't
seem to know any of them either. We walked up to Joe Landis,
Jessie's brother, and shook his hand.

"Thanks for coming," he said, in that hushed voice that
everyone uses in funeral homes.

"How are you holding up, man?" I asked.

Joe shook his head slightly, "Still in shock. I guess it really hasn't hit me yet."

"I don't see Charlie," said Linda, "I thought he'd be here."

I looked around, "He asked me about coming here yesterday at work, so I figured he'd be here, too."

At that point we were all asked to be seated, and the service began. The minister seemed to have at least a passing familiarity with Jessie, sighting a couple of stories about her youth activities at the church, which, quite frankly, surprised me, another side of Jessie revealed!

The service was over in a few minutes, and we all got up and moved out of the room while the funeral director began preparations for the ride to the cemetery.

Just then Jessie's mom, who had been sitting quietly next to Joe, yelled, "It was the devil! DEVILS killed my baby!!"

It was as if she suddenly became aware of where she was, or what was happening. Joe grabbed for her, but missed, as she ran to the casket and pounded on it, screaming:

"Your Grandfather is in league with devils, and one of his devils killed you, Jessica!!" I was at Joe's side by then, thinking maybe I could help, but mother Landis turned and looked me straight in the eye and yelled, "It was YOU! You were with her. *You're* the devil!"

"Oh great," I muttered, "someone else who thinks I did it!"

Joe grabbed me by the arm.

"Don't worry about her, man, she's not in our orbit. She's off in her little world. Hell, she doesn't even know who I am".

He moved to her side and tried to calm her as best he could, but she was really wound up now, and kept shrieking the word DEVILS. The small crowd was totally stunned by all this, and the funeral director was standing by the coffin probably wondering who to call to deal with this sort of disturbance.

At this point I caught a look at Talbert, who was giving me the evil eye, which I figured was only reasonable under the circumstances. He was standing next to Linda, and had probably been talking to her, before my accusation became the point of conversation. I was sweating nervously now, not from guilt, of course, but from embarrassment. I was actually a low profile kind of guy, in spite of my chosen career, and being the center of attention in a situation like this made me *really* uncomfortable!

Linda lunged toward me and said, "Let's get out of here! NOW!"

"I'm with you."

We headed for the door as Talbert, bless his heart, blocked our exit momentarily, saying, "I'm watching you Chandler, or whatever the hell your name is, a *lot* of people are watching you, so you better watch your step!"

I didn't bother to reply, but ran out to the car with Linda and got in.

Just as I started the Toronado, I heard the unmistakable rumbling of a Harley-Davidson. I looked in the rear view mirror and saw the same biker we saw earlier sitting right behind the car. The soaking wet rider was glaring in my direction. "Where are your friends?" I wondered aloud, as Linda closed her door and looked back, as well.

"Oh my GOD!" she exclaimed. "What in the hell is going on? I feel like Alice in Wonderland, none of this makes any sense!"

At that point the other bikes showed up.

The bikers gunned their engines and pulled out of the parking lot in formation, and drove away.

As we sat for a second to get our bearings back, I thought about what Carl Marchek had said. "Holy crap," I muttered, "this might be beginning to make sense, after all."

"How so?" said Linda.

"Everybody's looking for something, they all think I know where and what it is, and these guys are just the latest to come to the party. I believe Jessie was up to her pretty pink ass in drugs, and everyone seems to think I was in it with her."

"Do you know anything?"

"I can't say, but I think I might know enough to be in real danger!"

I backed out of the parking spot and headed out of the parking lot, "Would you like to take a ride to Toledo with me?"

"Sure, Why?"

"I want to find out about these Paladins. A friend of mine at WCWA can dig up info on anybody. We used to work together, he's a great investigator."

Linda paled and said, "You aren't going to try anything with them are you?"

"No, I'm not that crazy, but I do want to know who I'm dealing with, and if they're watching me... or watching US? I mean they knew I was driving your mom's car!"

Linda moaned, slumped in her seat, and muttered, "Damn it all, Jessie!"

The ride to Toledo was a short one, and I rather figured it would be uneventful.

Wrong again!

We were just past Nadeau Rd., near Monroe, when the bikes appeared behind us. They must have watched us leave the funeral home and stayed back far enough that I couldn't see them in the pouring rain. Then when we headed south on 75, they knew we were going to Toledo.

They stayed behind us in their usual formation riding through the rain. I joked it was the probably the closest they had been to a shower in ages. After a few minutes, they swept past us and continued on southward, leaving me wondering what the hell was going to happen next.

We exited the expressway and headed down Huron St. into a parking garage I had been a client of for several years past. It was located just behind the building containing WCWA AM and FM, and the studios of WTOL TV. I started my career there, and still had a fondness in my heart for the place. We entered through an almost invisible side door, which only some employees had a key for... I had "forgotten" to turn mine in when I left for Indiana. The station's Program Director, Barry Mills, had given me my first job in radio in '63, when I was still in high school. He greeted me with his usual enthusiasm, and smiled lasciviously at Linda saying, "Is this the future Mrs. Chandler?"

Linda and I smiled and said almost in unison, "we'll see". I then asked him if George Hoff was in the station, fortunately he was, and we went down the hall to the newsroom. George was sitting at a desk with his feet up, smoking a cigarette, and looking at a TV carrying the Channel 11 noon news.

"Hey Jeff, how are things at the Big 8?"

"Great," I said, "George, this is Linda. Linda, George." Brief handshakes and smiles followed, and George said, "What brings you to the old neighborhood, business or just passing through to make us jealous?"

"I stopped by to see what you know about a local motorcycle gang called the Paladins."

George looked concerned. "The Paladins? I know they're the kind of guys you want to stay away from! They're into drugs and all kinds of shit. They have a clubhouse out on Dorr Street. The cops are really going ape about them. They're supposed to be involved in everything short of human sacrifices, according to them. Why are you interested in them?"

"They seem to be interested in me, or should I say, *us*," I replied. I turned and closed the door to the newsroom, and continued, "There was a drug related murder in Detroit, and now a bunch of people think we must be involved since we knew the victim."

"Oh shit, sounds like you guys need to talk to the cops, quick!"

"Won't do much good," I answered. "The cops think I'm involved, too."

TWENTY–SIX
Back Home Again

"What?"

I gave George a brief summary of the investigation so far. He was surprised to learn I was still a suspect. "This guy's a real jackoff, isn't he?"

"Yeah, but he's tenacious. He's probably followed us here, too"

"Too?"

"Well, the bikers know we're headed to Toledo as well, even if they don't know we dropped by the station."

"This is starting to sound a bit dangerous. I know a few people at Toledo PD... maybe they can help."

"The real pain in the ass is that loudmouth cop," Linda complained, "it's getting to where we can't have any peace."

George smiled at her.

"Don't ask any questions," he said with a conspiratorial grin. "I think I've got an idea that will slow him down a bit."

"OK, just find out all the info you can get on those guys, huh?"

"Sure, Jeff, it was good to see you."

As Linda and I were leaving the building the same way we came in, through the side door, I heard another motorcycle. This one was a Toledo Police cycle, probably fresh from the Safety Building, just around the corner.

Good thinking, George, I thought, when the bike pulled up to Talbert's Ford, sitting in front of an expired meter, across Huron from the station. I had only suspected he had followed us to Toledo, having been a bit more concerned with the bikers at the

time. I realized he was sitting in the little White Tower burger
place on the corner of Huron and Jackson, waiting for Linda and
I to leave. I chuckled while one of Toledo's finest began writing
a citation for the offending car, although it was painfully obvious
that it was an unmarked police vehicle. Talbert came bellowing
out of the little restaurant with his badge out, and was starting to
give the traffic cop hell. As I grabbed Linda's arm and moved
into the parking garage, I found myself wondering if the cop was
going to give him an extra ticket for his belligerence.

"If we get out of here while he's busy, he'll never find us,
since he has no idea where he's going."

We retrieved the Toronado and pulled out onto the street
where Talbert was standing red-faced and looking nearly
apoplectic while the cop calmly continued to write on his pad.
As we pulled alongside I recognized the cop as an old high
school buddy, Phil Hayes.

"Hey Phil," I called out, "how's it goin'?"

"Jesus, Jeff Chandler! Hey, man, it's good to see you."

"How's business?" I asked with a grin.

He chuckled and winked. "Seems to be picking up."

"I see you landed a big one, man, don't give him up without
a fight,"

I smiled at Talbert. "Hey Sarge, welcome to Toledo. Maybe
you're the one that ought to watch your step. Hey, better yet,
maybe you should head on home."

I figured he wasn't going anywhere for a little while, since
his car was blocked by Phil's motorcycle in front, and another
parked car in the rear. But if *looks* could kill...

Having cut our police tail, our next stop was to visit with my
oldest friend in the world, David Mullins. We had known each
other since kindergarten at Longfellow school many years
before. We were like brothers. I was an only child and he only
had just a younger sister. We had both gravitated toward radio,
but in different ways.

Dave was an electronic genius, and became a ham radio
operator, while I wanted to be a disc jockey. At one point Dave
built a small broadcast transmitter, which allowed me to
broadcast from my bedroom "studio" over an area of about 3
blocks. It was a start.

These days Dave was kind of floundering, as he hadn't
found his calling in the real world, and was tending bar at a

neighborhood bar, *Benny's Bull Fiddle*, where most of our friends used to hang out.

As we walked through the door I said to Linda, "If I had all the money I've spent in here I could *buy* this dump! Then I'd fire that bum behind the bar and make him go out and get a *real* job."

The place was almost empty, so Dave greeted me with a genial, "Fuck off, Chandler."

"Hello, brother-I-never-had. How's it going?"

"Never better, and who is this vision of loveliness who deserves much better than you?"

"Linda, meet my unofficial brother. David, this is Linda Stevenson. She's hanging out with me until someone decent comes along to save her."

"Save me, save me!" Linda cried, clasping her hands together under her chin, rolling her eyes upward like a silent-film damsel in distress.

We all had a chuckle.

"Nice to see you buddy, it's been a while."

"Well it's been a strange couple of months. I mean *really* strange, give us a couple of beers and I'll fill you in on some of it."

After listening to the strange, twisted, tale, Dave shook his head.

"You guys need a place to hide? Nobody will look for you at my place."

"I appreciate it, buddy, but we have to get back, and I really don't think hiding out will help get this thing solved."

"But it could get you *killed!*"

"Nah, I'm too young and handsome to die... OK, maybe that's too young and stupid."

Linda suppressed a laugh, then took my arm. "OK, young man, let's hit the road, it's been a long, strange day and I'm getting hungry, and not just for food!"

"Some guys have all the luck," said Dave, "you always get the prettiest ones!"

Linda grinned and said "Don't worry, David, I'm sure to come back after I ditch this loser."

"Hey, Jeff... did she meet Mom? Oh, that's right, she's on vacation."

Ordinarily I would have dropped in to see my mom, but she was currently basking in the Hawaiian sun with her aunt Margie.

The two of them made a grand excursion every couple of years. Aunt Margie had never married, and since mom was the only widow among her nieces and nephews they traveled together. Aunt Margie was a wealthy woman, and enjoyed sharing with her family.

But Dave's question gave me an idea. I was a bit hungry myself.

"Hey, why don't we swing by my house here? I'm sure we can find something over there to… nibble on?"

"Lead on, Mac Duff."

It was pretty late before we made it back to the Motor City.

Twenty–Seven

(Jingle) More Music… C K L W, the Motor City.
Brad: *9:23 at the big 8 with Brad Walker on another rainy*
Monday morning with music by Archie Bell and the Drells.
Song: *Tighten Up.*

Allan held his hands up swinging an imaginary steering
wheel, suggesting I left a little gap, between where I stopped
talking, and the vocal began, (enough to drive a truck through).

"Speaking of the 'Tighten up'…" he said laughing.

I held up an unimaginary single finger.

"Say, Brad, what's the deal between you and Charlie?"

His question surprised me.

"What do you mean?"

"Well, for the last couple of weeks, you two have barely said
a thing to each other. Usually, you guys have something going
all the time. We've had a beer or two at Sid's, or at your place a
couple of times, with no sign of Charlie."

"Oh, I don't know, maybe he's taking Jessie's death a bit
hard. I think he was really starting to feel strongly about her."

"Yeah, maybe. But it isn't just… listen, maybe I'm just
imagining the whole thing, but it seems like you two don't really
trust each other like you used to.

"I know you said you've been thinking about who killed that
girl, and I was wondering if you're thinking of Charlie as a
suspect. I mean, he did know the girl. When was the last time
he saw her?"

"No, no," I protested, "I know Charlie couldn't have done
it."

But I had no idea when Charlie had seen Jessie last. We
never talked about her at all. Come to think about it, maybe I
didn't want to ask any questions. Charlie was a good friend, and
I didn't want to suspect him… did that mean I really *did* suspect
him.

Looking at it objectively, Charlie was as good a suspect as any. We all made OK money, but even if he only used a few pills and smoked a little grass, he dealt with people in the illegal drug business and if he was spending enough on his habit, he might have been willing to work with Jessie, or vice versa. He knew the girl and she probably wouldn't have suspected him if he wanted to meet.

He could also fit into a jealousy motive. There was that thing when Jessie came to my place the week before. He could have seen that as her sneaking around behind his back, I suppose. I mean, you wouldn't think he would have any sense of them being exclusive, but sometimes these things work like a burning fuse. I still didn't want to suspect Charlie, but maybe I had been doing it subconsciously.

"Maybe he suspects you?"

Maybe Allan was right. Even though we were friends, we did have reasons to be suspicious of each other when a girl we both knew turned up dead. We were afraid to talk about it and had let that wary suspicion grow into a barrier between us.

I was asked to introduce the Motown Monday program at the Rooster Tail that night. Linda backed out at the last minute, so I was on my own for the evening.

On my way in, I saw our friend Talbert in the crowd. I was fairly certain he hadn't bird-dogged me there. Maybe he was just a Motown fan, maybe he was working on another case.

After I did my bit, the first person I ran across was Bruce Cole, my mid- morning counterpart at WKNR. Keener had been the number one station in Detroit until we came along, and had just recently knocked them off their perch. Cole was really a kind of dull person and, I have to admit, I'd usually try to avoid a conversation, but since I had found that Jessie had worked at KNR as a Kelly girl…

"Hey, Walker, how are you?"

"Hello, Bruce."

Cole wasn't very dynamic, but he had a real salesman's handshake.

"I heard you were seeing that girl they found in the river. I was sorry to hear that. I don't know if you knew, but she worked at our station for a few weeks. She seemed like a nice girl."

"Yeah, we were friends."

"If there anything is we can do for you, let me know, huh?"

"Sure."

I tried to make it casual.

"Used to work there, eh?"

"Yeah. She was quite a looker. To be honest with you, I took a bit of a run at her myself, but she didn't seem interested."

Not a big surprise, but then again she did have a shower with Chucklehead, who was no smooth operator, either. Then again maybe he was just a convenient foil for her shower performance, as opposed to a person she would spend an evening with.

"All the guys took notice of her."

"She click with anybody else?"

"No, not that I knew of. She was only there a couple of months. There was a rumor she did one of the jocks during his show, but I figure that was just rumor because she was, you know... flirty with all the guys."

Well, based on my experience, it was possible, but since he didn't give me a name, I had nothing to go on.

I nodded for his benefit.

We had one of those awkward silent moments.

"Have a good night, Brad."

"Good night."

The night was almost over when I spotted Ferante's right hand man, Michael Lang. I followed him through the crowd until he ended up at a table occupied by Mitchell Martin and *Talbert?* Martin and Talbert were deep in conversation and barely acknowledged Lang when he greeted them. I found myself thinking about what the old man said about cops being in business for themselves. Were Talbert and Martin business partners? Was Talbert investigating him? Were they friends, or just a pair of cops sharing war stories?

(Jingle)And the hits just keep on coming... C-K-L-W, the Motor City.

It's 8:00 at the Big 8 on a hot Tuesday evening, Brad Walker filling in for superstar Tim Sheldon...

Six to nine *pm* was the most popular slot in those radio days. People still sometimes opted for radio over the five or six TV channels they had to view. It was the big stage for a radio guy.

It had been a while since I had got a chance to sit in the big chair. After three hours of playing hits, and talking to listeners, I headed home.

I had just gotten comfortable in my recliner and started my second cold Labatt's Blue, when the phone rang.

"Brad? Oh, thank god you're home. You've got to help, I'm in deep trouble. Can you meet me?"

"Linda? Calm down, where are you?"

"I'm at Sid's."

"Sid's? Women aren't allowed at Sid's"

"I'm here already. Don't worry, I'm dressed as a guy."

"Well, that doesn't sound like trouble."

"Just come and get me, huh?"

"Yeah, on the way."

TWENTY—EIGHT
Damsel in distress

```
Run for your life if you can little girl.
        —Run for Your Life, the Beatles
```

As I got to Sid's, Bob, the Beer Man, met me in the lobby.

"Over in the left corner," he said in his Glaswegian brogue. "You've got to get her out of here, Mr. Walker! You know women aren't allowed in the bar, not even... under camouflage."

I nodded.

"It isn't that I care meself, but if the proprietor, or the LLBO spot her, it'll be my job."

"Didn't fool you a bit, did she?"

"Oh, she was a wee passable with her short hair and all, but that face and those eyes were a dead giveaway."

I nodded. "Look, Bob, I'm sorry about this... We'll be heading out. Do I at least have time for a pint?"

"Oh, aye" he nodded, his accent continuing to thicken.

I handed him a dime and took a draft ale from his tray.

"Don't worry, I'll have a word with 'him', Bob."

"Please. And the other lass as well?"

The what?

"The other girl? Jessie?" I was startled

"The blonde one. I don't think I knew her name. I remember her as one of your party last month. Normally I might not have, but we get so few women, and this one... well, she... handled my leg, if you know what I mean."

I tried and failed to suppress a chuckle, remembering her tendency to be a bit busy with her hands.

"She does that sort of thing," I tried to sound both calm and casual. "When was she here?"

"Tuesday, couple weeks back."

"June 4th?" *That couldn't be right.*

"No, end of May. What, 27th or so. I know for sure it were last Tuesday in May."

That was interesting. If she was on this side of the river, why didn't she call me, or leave a note or something? I was her big hero, wasn't I? She could have picked up her car. If she didn't want me involved, she shouldn't have left the car and if she did mean to involve me, she should have been in touch.

But if she was here, she had to be trying to meet someone and avoid recognition at the same time. But somebody must have known who she was.

Come to think of it, with her car on this side, how did she manage to get back over here?

"She was a wee easier to spot," Bob said. A smile crossed his face in spite of himself.

I thought about that package of Marilyn Monroe curves she had and grinned.

"She tried the same camouflage with a big shirt and loose coat, but she's got tits 'til Tuesday, if you don't mind me saying."

She would have loved that description.

"So, did she meet somebody here?"

"Don't know, sir. She sort of slipped in, like this one, but I finished my tour around, you know, and was going to have a wee word the next time, but she was already gone. She was nae here but a minute or two."

She met someone here while disguised. Apparently by plan. So whoever she met might have wanted her to not be recognized either.

I couldn't resist stirring the pot a bit in the end.

"I'll have a word with them Bob, but you need to know, these American girls have really got equal rights on the brain. You're lucky they haven't started organizing protests."

"Oh, aye," he acknowledged. "but I still need to do me job, and follow the law. Your American girls are about to be the death of me."

"Know what you mean, Bob."

Linda was in the booth, back near the darkest corner of the place, sort of huddled down. Her beer was on the table but barely touched. As Bob said, she wasn't too obvious at first glance and distance, but there was little doubt when you saw her face in profile.

A couple of guys near her had taken a second look and either guessed the truth or were simply puzzled and were sort of casting quick glances her way. One guy shot me a conspiratorial grin.

She looked up just as I got to the table, and to her credit, she, although tempted to jump into my arms, made no physical movement toward me.

She looked back down at the table as I slid in across the booth.

"Thank god you're here." She said, softly.

"This is a bad idea, Linda," I said bluntly, "and not a very good masquerade."

"I had to. They were looking for a woman. I figured nobody would look for me in a place like this, let alone dressed like this."

I wondered if Jessie had thought the same thing. The disturbing thing is 'they' seemed to have found her anyway.

"Who's looking for you," I asked.

"I don't know, the people who killed Jessie I suppose."

...Or the cops, or the organization.

"Do you know who 'they' are?"

"No." She looked at me intently. "I'm serious. I really have no idea. The cops think Jessie gave me something, or told me something about who killed her, but she didn't... I don't *know* anything."

"How do you know these guys are after you?"

"I haven't *seen* them if that's what you mean. But somebody went through my house and wrecked it! They tore up parts of the floor and punched holes in the wall and left everything everywhere. As far as I can tell, they didn't take anything, but it just scared the shit out of me. They must have been looking for whatever it is that Jessie was supposed to have."

"What? What is it she was supposed to have?"

"Damn it, Brad, you don't believe me either! I was... I came here hoping you would help me, but you're just like everybody else."

"Hey! Just calm down, huh?"

She was partially right. I did think she knew what Jessie was up to, it was quite possible she was holding out on me and either had something or knew what it could have been. On the other hand, she might know something and not realize what she knows. Then, she could also be in business for herself and playing me for a sucker. But even if I thought she was flat out lying, I had little doubt that dangerous people were after her.

The biggest question was, could I protect her? Or would I just be putting my own head under a bus and about to be the next guy caught floating in the river. Could I trust her?

"Look, I don't know if I *can* help, but I haven't drawn any conclusions, yet.

"Your house? Did you call the police."

"Police? And tell them what?"

"You could have told them your house was vandalized. That would have worked for a start."

"But once they found out who I was, they would find out about Jessie and then all I would get is a lot more suspicion."

"Yeah, I suppose," I said, not completely convinced.

I drained my beer in a few gulps. "OK, let's go."

"So you believe me?"

"We can't stay here," I said, ignoring the question, "we're breaking the law."

TWENTY-NINE

I fought the law and the law won.
    —I Fought The Law, Bobby Fuller Four

Talbert and RCMP Sgt. McGowan were waiting for me in the lobby of the Holiday Inn.

"We've got you this time, Bucko," Talbert snarled.

"Good afternoon," I said, as coolly as I could.

McGowan shot the Detroit cop a look. Reminding him whose territory he was infringing on, I suppose.

"We're sorry to disturb you, Mr…"

"Walker will work just fine." I acknowledged.

"We have a bit of a problem. Would you come with us, please?"

"Sure."

They led me out into the parking lot and Jessie's black Mustang.

"Do you recognize this car?" the Mountie asked.

I took a step or two closer as if I weren't certain.

"I'd just be guessing," I lied, "but it might be Jessie's."

"You knew where this car was all along!" Talbert accused.

"Wait a minute," I snapped back. "I just assumed the only black mustang with Michigan plates you would expect me to recognize would be Jessie's, but the truth was every time we went out one of the others did the driving. I never saw her in that car." *Genuine truth there.* "Why do you suppose she parked it here?"

"I guess we have to assume," McGowan said, "that she must have left it here the night you took her home."

"OK, after what happened that night she was too shaken to drive home. The makes sense," I nodded. "I take it you made sure it was hers. You know there should be a registration…"

I had checked. There hadn't been one.

"Oh, it's the right car alright," Talbert said.

"There is one thing we aren't too sure about," McGowan said, opening the trunk.

Bobby Charlton lay curled up on the trunk floor, with a small hole in the right side of his head. I don't think it was the surprise, or even the sight that got to me. It was the incredible and unmistakable smell that set me to immediate retching.

Neither cop seemed particularly sympathetic with my reaction. In fact, Talbert seemed almost amused.

"Do you know this man?" McGowan asked.

I nodded. "His name is Bobby Charlton."

"You admit you know him?" Talbert was surprised.

"He's a backer of a couple of local music groups and an investor in at least one studio. He's also, rumor has it, a big time drug dealer."

"What makes you think he's a drug dealer?" McGowan asked.

I shrugged.

"Don't you think it's an interesting coincidence that you know two people, both possibly involved with drugs and both dead?"

"…but, of course, you wouldn't know any thing about that, would you," Talbert grumbled.

"They are also both involved with this car, aren't they? It might not be completely coincidental, but it's pretty obvious that Charlton wasn't killed at the same time Jessie was nor that he was in the trunk when she brought the car here."

"Why would you say that?" McGowan asked.

"It's been a couple of weeks since Jessie's body was discovered, and she was dead a week or so before that. I'm no expert, but if he'd been in the trunk that long, he'd look a lot worse, wouldn't he?"

Plus, I knew he wasn't in that trunk a week ago.

"Maybe *you* killed him?" Talbert poked.

"I thought I was supposed to have killed Jessie? So now I killed this Charlton in revenge? Then maybe left his dead body at my own front door… perhaps to avoid suspicion?"

McGowan smiled broadly.

"If we assume Jessie was working with somebody trying to cut Charlton out of the deal," I said, "his murder would fit easily into the category of a takeover, right?"

"Either the competition or an internal coup, eh?"

"Sure, and Jessie's car is a convenient blind alley. Only tangentially related to her murder, but with enough suspects, including me, to keep the waters murky until they complete their takeover."

"Not to mention," McGowan said, "If Charlton's people get rid of you, everybody might consider the whole thing case closed."

Great, I hadn't thought of that yet.

"My question is, how did whoever it was know where to find Jessie's car? Who would even be looking?"

"Maybe she had something valuable in the car... money or maybe drugs."

"But she had a couple of days to get the car if she left it that Saturday. It would have been either her profit or her life insurance. Why wouldn't she have secured it?"

"Because," Talbert sneered, "her boyfriend was keeping it for her."

"Sure, you believe that... that's why you've been following Linda this whole time." I shook my head. "No, wait a minute—prove I've been keeping the car. Did you fingerprint it?"

"Actually we did," McGowan said "Somebody seems to have wiped the car clean."

"Clean?" I reacted a bit to that one. I knew I kept my prints off the thing, but somebody clearly must have cleaned it between the murders.

"Inside and outside?" I asked.

"Yeah."

"He washed and waxed a car in the parking lot of the Holiday Inn? That seems risky to me."

"Not if he lived there," Talbert said.

"You keep playing that same note—it's flat already. People here know me... *and* my car. They would surely notice me washing *someone else's* car, wouldn't they?"

"Good point, I suppose," McGowan said. "You're suggesting that he took the car, then brought it back?"

It suddenly registered that the car may have indeed been moved a space or two, but I hadn't been that certain of the original location.

"I don't think anyone could just shoot him in the head already in a car trunk in the Holiday Inn parking lot, could they? The scene in that trunk would also be messier, wouldn't it?

They killed him somewhere else. Putting the body in the car here is just a convenient way to keep all eyes on me."

I anticipated Talbert's next argument.

"Yeah, yeah, Sarge. It could all have just been done by me, but the same objections apply. If my car was here and her car was here, how did I ever move the body? And like I keep saying… people here know my car. They would remember me driving something else."

The good news was they were still questioning me down at the car. Although my logic was impeccable, I could never convince them of my innocence if they ever searched the apartment and found any of the keys that were up there—the five of cocaine, or the two to Jessie's car. Especially since one key fit the trunk.

Finding Linda would have complicated the thing, too. But we could probably explain that, if necessary.

"Maybe it's nothing, but she did send a message to somebody here in Windsor."

I told them what I had learned at the front desk without explaining the conclusions I had drawn.

"Been investigating on your own?" McGowan asked with a sort of friendly smile.

I shrugged. "Just trying to make a little sense of the whole thing."

"The Landis killing is Detroit's jurisdiction," he said, "but this one seems to point to you more than a bit, you have a strong possible revenge motive…"

"…but there's no evidence to connect me. You're saying don't leave the area?"

"Don't leave the area."

"Can't you lock him up?" Talbert whined

"Oh, come on," I said. "You want me on the streets… maybe I'll do my next killing right in the hotel lobby so you'll have witnesses."

McGowan laughed out loud. "We really don't gain much by locking him away at this point," he pointed out. "We might have enough suspicion to hold him, but we have absolutely no evidence to substantiate a charge."

"Don't worry, I said," grinning at Talbert. "I'm not leaving town… this time." He glared angrily at me. "How did you like Toledo, anyway?"

When I got up to the apartment, I was looking forward to telling Linda how close she had come to being found out, but she wasn't there.

No note.

No message!

Just *poof.*

My heart sank. She had come across the border afraid people were after her. I humored her, but I really didn't take her seriously. Now, suddenly, it not only looked like she was right after all, but that her pursuers had found her. On the other hand, there was no sign of force or struggle around the apartment, she just wasn't there. Maybe she got a little stir crazy and decided to get out of the room for a while. Figuring the border kept her safe from harm, maybe she wanted to get out a bit.

I decided she would be back in a little while and we'd laugh over my worries.

While I was relaxing in the lounge chair, I speculated about who might really be after her. There was clearly no shortage of suspects. Charlton or Ferante might have grabbed her thinking she knew something about Jessie's contacts. The Bikers, assuming they were the other end, might think she had the drugs or money. All of them, including the Mob, might grab her if they thought I knew something and realized they could get to me through her.

But the real chilling thought was if she had fallen in the hands of Jessie's killer or a sadist like Mitchell Martin.

The police could provide little help. Not only would they have a lot of questions I'm not sure I could answer and several I'm not sure I'd want to. There was, as far as I could tell, little evidence to whittle down the list of potential suspects. Besides, these are incredibly ruthless people, who might choose to just kill her. The cops trying to save her might put her in greater peril than she was already in.

I fell asleep waiting to hear something. I woke when Mac came in.

"You're not waiting up for me?" he asked.

"Linda's gone."

"Gone, what do you mean gone? She was staying here because she was in danger wasn't she? She was here when I left tonight at about 7:30. Did you check for her car in the lot?"

"No. Come to think of it, I don't even know if her car is here. Besides, I probably shouldn't be prowling the parking lot looking for cars today, anyway."

I told him about Jessie's car and Charlton's body, but not about my prior discovery of the Mustang. It suddenly struck me that I needed to check my 'golf clubs' to see if Linda might not have found the evidence. Mac agreed the cops might still be watching the lot.

"Makes sense. Maybe Linda saw the cops and figured they'd get around to searching the place, so she decided to slip out before that happened."

That idea hadn't occurred to me. It sounded right, but you would think she'd call to see if the coast was clear. Or maybe she thought they were still watching the place, too.

"She'll probably call or come back in the morning." He concluded.

But the morning brought no new news at all.

THIRTY
Searching

```
I can't see me lovin' nobody but you, for
all my life.
                    —The Turtles, Happy Together
```

"CKLW request line…"

"Can you play 'Happy Together' by the Turtles?"

I knew that voice. "Hello Casey… must be a slow day at work."

"Hi, Jeff… No it's OK. The girls here just wanted to hear a song and I wanted to remind you that Mark and Debbie were coming up from Ft. Wayne tomorrow."

"Tomorrow…" I had completely forgotten about it, and with Linda's disappearance occupying my mind…

"Oh, Brad… You didn't make plans did you?"

I couldn't very well back out on the possibility that I *might* have to go searching for Linda *in case* she's in danger."

"No… it's nothing like that. I'll be there in the morning."

Provided nothing happened, of course.

"You OK, you sound strange."

"No, I'm good Case, see you in the morning."

"Bye."

Mac walked into the studio.

"You heard the news, right?"

"News?"

Mac looked at Allan, who shrugged. "I figured Charlie said something, so I didn't."

Charlie had said practically nothing that morning, and I have to admit, I was sort of musing on the idea that perhaps we both considered the other to be a suspect.

"Bennett Cole."

"Cole, the overnight board operator? What happened to him?"

"Windsor Police came and arrested him during his shift. Took him out of the building in cuffs. Left Campbell running his own board. Greg ended up coming in about an hour earlier than usual. Believe it or not, the union might file a grievance."

"Grievance?" I started, then saw Mac's smirk and realized he was just yanking my chain.

"What did they arrest him for?"

"All kinds of rumor, but the latest I heard was he was busted for selling coke."

"Cole was a coke dealer?"

"Apparently."

I remembered that Jessie spent some time chatting with Cole several times during the party we had for Chuckles, including right before telling Linda she had a source for coke. Could that have been Cole? Maybe he was the missing link in the drug smuggling conspiracy? But even if he knew something, how was I going to get any information out of him when he was in police hands?

"So, is this the lead story on 20/20 news?"

"No, but I think the *Windsor Star* is going to make good mileage out of that. Drugs at CKLW, the evil influence of rock and roll and all of those Americans infiltrating the place, that sort of foolishness."

"I don't know, it might be a big thing if it was somebody on the air, but I don't think they'd get a lot of interest from the public about somebody they had never heard of."

Mac nodded. "I guess you're right. Still no word from Linda?"

I had checked my hiding place and made certain Jessie's bundle was still intact, so it seemed unlikely she was out trying to take up where Jessie left off.

"Not a word," I answered. "This afternoon, I'm going to head over to her place."

"You think she just went home?"

"No, but what else have I got go on?"

"Maybe you got a point."

RCMP Sgt. McGowan caught me in the parking lot.

"I figured going in might start rumors after yesterday." He said with a cheerful smile.

"Yeah, but if you just keep hanging out in places waiting for me wouldn't that start entirely different rumors?"

He laughed.

"You heard about Bennett Cole, I suppose?"

"I heard he was arrested."

"Thought you'd want to know what he told us about Jessie Royce."

"Did he confirm your suspicion about her being involved in drugs?"

"Sort of, he told us he sold her half a kilo."

"That's a big quantity," I said. "But probably insignificant in the border traffic. Too small for any of the major players to be concerned."

"Also, it's retail grade. Other than split it, there wasn't much she could do with it. She would want to have access to better grade stuff."

"Is Cole significant in the drug business? Could he have been getting ambitions and was using Jessie to broker a deal?"

"And he paid her in coke up front? Again, why? And it's the wrong direction, too. The coke is coming into Canada, and she's smuggling it back into the US."

"Talbert would say she left it here for me."

McGowan looked at me a moment. "Yeah, but I know better."

I let it sit there, but there was something a little disconcerting about how certain he was.

"So what does that mean?"

He shook his head. "The Royce murder is a Detroit police matter. We'll pass on what Cole told us to Talbert, but if it were me, I'd have to reconsider my suspect list for a more personal motive for the murder."

As I was cruising out toward Grosse Pointe Farms it struck me that my arrival out there might be a bit awkward. I had never met any of Linda's family except for her little sister, under sort of embarrassing circumstances. So what was I going to tell them?

She was missing? They'd have the cops there in a heartbeat.

We had a date? They'd expect me to wait, but for how long?

That old cliché... I was just in the neighborhood?

Still, as I told Mac, I really couldn't think of much else to do.

I was surprised to find Linda's door partially open as I parked my car on the driveway. I know she said someone ransacked her place, but it would be mostly instinctive to close the door, wouldn't it?

As I passed cautiously through her rooms, I heard music splashing and laughter from the pool area.

She was having a party?

After all the aggravation I've been going through...

Just then one of the boys that had crashed our little pool party a few weeks before came walking into the place on his way to the bathroom, I suppose. He was at least wearing trunks this time. Little Sister was throwing a pool party. But Linda had said people were taking care of her, and I don't think they had called for a party.

"Good afternoon," I said.

He blinked, then smiled in recognition. "hiya," he answered without breaking stride.

Linda's sister Brandy was perched on a barstool in a yellow floral print two-piece suit. Although a bit more conservative than her sister's blue suit, it was still pretty revealing for a 16-year old.

"Ooh! Brad Walker..." She peeled herself from the stool and ambled toward me, adjusting her suit in that way women do to remind observers how barely covered they are.

"Lin's not here, stud," she moved in close. "but you're welcome to stay and take a dip." She grinned wickedly.

I caught a solid whiff of beer.

"You're drunk," I noticed.

She smiled crookedly. "Who are you, my mother? Or maybe you want to be Daddy... is that it, want to turn me over your knee and spank me?"

I started laughing. She was trying to play older and seduce me. Unlike some girls her age, she had all the right equipment for the job, but she just didn't have the experience to pull it off.

"Actually, kid, I was just looking for your sister."

"She actually hasn't been home for a couple of days. Maybe you've been replaced?"

I couldn't think of any comment or answer that wouldn't raise an alarm over her disappearance. So I said:

"Maybe. When she gets home have her give me a call, huh?"

As I began to pull away, Brandy raced out to my car.

"Hey," she called, "Is Lin in any trouble?"

"I really don't know." I answered. "She was just going to stop by yesterday, but she didn't make it."

"Don't give me that! You're really worried, aren't you?"

"Look, it's probably nothing..." I tried to reassure her.

"Listen, seriously, I might have an idea where she might hide out if she's in some kind of bad trouble. A place in the city."

"Hey... I can't..."

"Look, she's my sister, and I want to find her as bad as you do. Just give me a few minutes to get rid of these guys and throw some clothes on."

She raced off toward the house.

Linda might be in danger, I thought, but there was plenty of evidence that baby sister here was going to definitely be a source of trouble.

THIRTY—ONE
Veteran Observer

It was an itsy-bitsy teenie-weenie yellow polka
dot bikini…
—*Itsy-Bitsy Teenie-Weenie Yellow Polka Dot
Bikini*, Bryan Hyland

As I waited, the other teenagers emerged from Linda's
apartment and piled into a '62 Ford Fairlane that had been
stashed in Linda's spot in the garage. As they raced off, Linda's
little sister emerged in a schoolgirl white blouse and a just above
the knee black skirt. She had gone from *femme fatale* seductress
to plain Jane schoolgirl in about four minutes.

"I thought someone was keeping an eye on you," I noted as I
rolled out toward downtown.

"What do you care?"

I shrugged, "I don't. I was just curious."

"I do this all the time in the summer. I spend the weekend at
my friend Crystal's. We goof off wherever we want on Friday
'cause her folks think we're here and my folks think we're at her
place.

"Old lady Carson, our housekeeper, is deaf as a post and
loves her soap operas. So the two of us usually hang out at
Lin's. Today she wasn't even at the house because she's been
staying with me all week. She went home to boff the old man or
feed her cat."

"So since nobody was there to supervise…"

"Yeah, pool party."

Did you know Linda wasn't going to be home?" I asked.

No, I didn't, but it didn't matter. She wouldn't rat on us.
Besides, I know about all her moves and hangouts."

"How's that," I asked.

"Oh, she used to tell me everything, until she got kicked out
of college."

"Kicked out?" *Not the story I heard.*

"Yeah, she got into some kind of sorority trouble at Michigan and they 'asked her to leave,' since then, she doesn't tell me shit, so I follow her. In my car."

"She never noticed?"

"Not as far as I can tell. Jessie knew, though. I think she enjoyed the attention. Sometimes, after Lin gave me the slip, Jessie would tell me where they went and what they did."

I shook my head, beginning to have some idea why a sixteen year-old might be drinking in the middle of the afternoon.

"So where are we going?"

"Lin and Jessie used to visit this house sometimes down in the city. Nobody would look for either of them there because it's mostly... I mean, it's sort of a black neighborhood, but not so black that they would stand out."

The gray duplex was on 21st street, just north of Porter almost at the entrance to the Ambassador Bridge.

"They used to visit the guy who lives upstairs." She said.

"You've seen this guy?"

"Yeah, hair cut like a soldier, big like you, nice muscles."
Matt Royce?

OK. You stay here."

"But, Brad..."

"Look, we've got enough trouble without getting you involved any further. I'm just going to ask if she's there. If the coast is clear, I'll let you know. If there's any kind of trouble. You've got to go for help, right? It's important."

"Trouble, what kind of trouble?"

"You just never know." I wasn't really anticipating any trouble, but I figured she would be more likely to stay there if she had a duty to perform.

"If anything bad happens, kid, start the car and get out of here. The Police station is down on Fort Street."

Her eyes widened. Then she sort of pouted.

"OK," she said hesitantly.

I got a couple of steps.

"Hey, Walker?"

"Yeah."

"Be careful, huh?"

He ain't home," a voice from the other door said.

I turned to see an old black woman emerge from the lower unit.

"You looking for Mr. Rice, he just left for the store."

"Oh." I hadn't really come up with a reason to explain my visit to anyone other than the guy who lived there, so I struggled for a second to think of something.

"A, uh, friend of mine asked me to stop by because I was going to be passing through today. I guess I'll try to stop by later.

She looked me over carefully. "He don't really get many visitors," she said. "He has a girlfriend that comes by sometimes, but she hasn't stopped over in a while."

I nodded and continued to listen. "Very nice young man, quiet as a mouse. Last fellow thumped and thundered around loud enough to wake the dead."

"He's going to the store, on a bad leg you know, but he stops by and knocks. 'Mrs. Berry,' he says, 'Do you want anything from the market?' I loaned him my little shopping cart, and off he went."

"Does he go to the store often?"

No. His girlfriend usually goes to market for him, but the last couple of weeks, the other lady in the fancy car has been doing it."

"What kind of car is it?"

"Lord, I don't know those things… just red. Julius, my nephew, might know if you want to call him."

I shook that off.

"In fact, she stopped by yesterday for a hot minute."

"She was by yesterday? Did she forget the groceries?"

"Don't know. She stopped by a little after noon, like I said, a hot minute, then gone."

She looked at me "Do you know her?"

"Well, we've met," I answered vaguely'

She gave me a closer look.

"Are you with the Veterans'?"

"Ma'am?" I thought I looked a bit too young for a veteran, but I suppose there were guys my age who had been to 'Nam and back, and others who went to work for the government right out of school. It was actually a good cover story.

"You came to see how he's adjusting after his injuries?"

I nodded. "It's good to hear that he's getting around."

"He has nightmares… about the war and the fighting, I hear him sometimes. My husband, rest his soul, had the nightmares and night sweats for years after he came back from France too. He fought in the First World War, you know, nothing like the one on the evening news."

There was no question in my mind that the Mr. Rice who lived upstairs was the Matt Royce who slipped away from a military hospital.

"His leg was real bad, you know, when he came here. It's a little better lately."

That's why Jessie needed the coke she got from Bennett Cole.

"He still shouldn't be running around on it, especially as far as the store. I just don't think they did a great job of fixing it the first time. I really think he should be back in the hospital."

I nodded.

"If it was up to me,' I said with all honesty, "I'd put him in tomorrow. But the best I can do is recommend it."

Since Royce couldn't surface, it was up to Jessie to find a source of pain killers. That would explain how she met some of the players in the drug trade and perhaps how she got herself into the mess that killed her.

"Well, I'll try to stop by later. I have other people to see today."

I took a step or two. "It's probably best," I offered, "that he doesn't know we're checking up on him. We don't want him thinking that the Army is trying to control his life, you know Mrs…?"

"Berry, Katherine Berry, but everyone here calls me Mama K.

"Well, Mama, I'll probably be talking to you when I come back."

"Wasn't he home?" Brandy asked.

"No."

"So we wait?"

"No chance, our neighbor is pretty observant and I convinced her I had to go. Besides, she said Linda was here yesterday, but left."

"Left, going where?"

"Don't know yet, but you're going home."

"Home? But…"

"No buts. No need having both of you missing. Actually, you're off to your friend's house, right?"

"But Lin's still out there!"

"Any idea where?

"Well… No."

"Me neither, but I'm the one that has to figure that out. I also need to get you to someplace safe, because if she's in trouble, one of the easiest ways for someone to get her to do what they want is to grab *you*. So until we find her, you are going to be a *very* good girl. No hiding out or sneaking, no private pool parties, right?"

She glared at me, but eventually lowered her head. "OK, I guess."

She pouted all the way back to Grosse Pointe.

After dropping little sister off at her friend's house (at least I hoped it was!), I called back home to see if she had come back, or left a message. Not a word from Linda, but there *was* a call from my best friend since kindergarten.

Got your girl here, what do we do with her now?
                                    —Mullins

THIRTY—TWO
Meeting Paladin

12:27 at the Big 8, Big Bill Davis coming at you with music from Miss Fontella Bass.
(Music Up) Rescue me, and take me in your arms. Rescue me…

We?

Even before "What the hell is Linda doing in Toledo?", the pronoun Dave used caught my eye. Exactly who else made up the "we"?

Why would Linda go to Toledo? Wouldn't she, couldn't she, have at least let me know before heading out? Was she kidnapped from my place? Captured somewhere else? Or did she go there on her own?

Did she find Mullins, or did he happen upon her somehow? And of course, who the hell was *we*?

The miles flew by as the Cutlass rolled down the highway south toward home. But I was only thinking about the answers I would hopefully find when I got there.

It was about the cocktail hour when I got to the bar and found a parking spot.

When I got to the bar I saw Linda, as expected, sitting in a booth sipping a cocktail. The surprise, for me, was Carl Marchek sitting at the bar, nursing a beer. His presence indicated that he might be the rest of the 'we' Dave mentioned in his note.

"Hey, Jeff, good to see you again so soon," Dave said cheerily, turning to draw a beer for me.

"Dave, what the hell…"

The rest of my question was interrupted by Linda, who, seeing my arrival, sprang from her booth and clung to me, sobbing.

"She was at the Paladins' hideout last night," Dave explained, "When the police, or maybe it was the feds, raided the place. She got rolled up with all the bikers and chucked into jail. I got a phone call..." his head moved ever so slightly, but surely, toward Marchek. "...telling me she was in jail and so I went down to post bail for her. You owe me 50 bucks."

"Ah, what the hell," I said, with a wink, "you put up the money... just keep her."

Her head popped up from my shoulder and she looked narrowly at us both, then realized we were just joking, so she punched feebly at my chest and buried her head again, tightening her grip.

"I was so scared," she murmured into my clothes.

I peeled her loose. "How did you get yourself into this mess anyhow?"

"Somebody called, and told me the Paladins were after my little sister, Brandy..."

"I told you not to answer the phone. The desk would take any messages..." I stopped. It was a dumb argument to have.

"I know," she moaned, "but... anyway, I stopped by the house to make sure she was OK, but they must have been waiting for me.

"They brought me down here and held me against my will. They kept asking me questions about you and Jessie, but there wasn't anything I could tell them. I mean, we don't know anything, do we?"

I nodded sympathetically. She was preaching to the choir on that one.

"I was scared until the police arrived. Then they arrested *me* and threw me into jail with those revolting women who were drinking and smoking and doing drugs with those lowlifes. Fortunately, David here found out (he's very, very mysterious about how) and made arrangements for bail."

She sniffed and sort of wiped her face on my shirt.

Then stepped back, sort of covering her face. "I must look terrible," she said. "I think I'll go fix my face."

As she headed off to the Ladies' room, I moved down to the end of the bar.

"You had them staked out?" I asked Marchek

"Not exactly. The raid was planned, but we never expected the girl to be there."

"Doesn't that add kidnapping charges for our scumbag bikers?"

"Not really, all indications are that she walked in there voluntarily and was never restrained, at least not in any obvious fashion.

"In fact, we have a source that suggests she has at least some passing acquaintance with the head of the Paladins, a fellow who calls himself Pig Iron."

"Pig Iron?" I started chuckling.

"His real name is Stanley Wolarski, so I guess a nickname was in order, but it's bad, right? Pig Pen, like in the comics, maybe, or Scrap Iron, but Pig Iron is sort of ridiculous."

So Linda was a bit of a suspect after all.

"Does *she* know you're a Fed?"

"No, not yet. I told your pal the bartender and don't object to her knowing, but I'd rather it not become common knowledge."

Linda joined us.

"We're sitting at the bar now?"

"I was just here talking to Dave and…"

"Carl."

"Carl, here. We can go back to the table."

As we sat, Linda asked, "Carl another old friend?"

"Nah, just a fellow at the bar. He struck up a conversation, you know."

She smiled vaguely at me leaving me wondering if she suspected, or even knew, I was lying.

Time to change the subject. "I was worried about you, searching everywhere. How did they bring you down here?"

"They, uh, made me drive *my* car" she said hesitantly. "One of those… pigs sat on the other seat."

After the information I got from Marchek, I was feeling pretty skeptical about the whole tale, but figured I should get the entire version.

"So this guy left his Harley somewhere in Grosse Pointe Farms while he rode back to Toledo in your G.T.O."

She blinked and her eyes drifted upward as if thinking.

"How the hell should I know? Suddenly you don't believe me now?"

She was pretty defensive and hurt that I was asking questions about her version of events. But all the while I was feeling more skeptical.

"I was only thinking, that the cops up there might be able to spot the bike. Not only would it help identify your passenger, but it would help confirm your story to the Police.

"You really don't believe me! You think I'm making the whole thing up."

"Hey, *I'll* take your word for it," I answered. "But the people you have to convince are the police. Besides, that motorcycle is just the thing to give our Sgt. Talbert something more important to do than follow you around."

There was no mistaking her reaction to that one. She had done something recently that had her worried that she might have been followed. Was it her trip to Toledo (with or without biker escort)? or her quick visit to the mysterious Mr. Rice on 21st Street? Or was there something else...

She glared at me for a second while I drained the beer in front of me, and then gestured to Dave to bring me another. He drew one from the tap and set it on the bar with his own distinctive gesture suggesting it was going to be self-service (since I was getting them free)

"Such language," Linda giggled.

I retrieved the beer and returned to the booth.

"Want to shoot some pool?" she asked.

"Sure, if you want to," I answered.

"What are the stakes?" she asked. "Just to make things interesting?"

I'm a decent enough player, but I thought about my tour of her house and the custom-built billiard table in the game room.

"Sure as hell ain't playing for money," I said.

"Chicken?"

"Yep."

She thought for a moment, then an evil smile crossed her face. "Winner gets to screw the loser's brains out."

"Rack 'em."

THIRTY–THREE
A Shooting War

We were playing our third game (series one game each), when I looked up from the table and saw Linda turn as white as a ghost. I turned back toward the door and saw a man in his 30s. He didn't look that different from the other bar patrons except for his longer hair and the fact that I recognized him, having seen him in motorcycle gear at a funeral.

"Hiya, toots," he greeted Linda.

I stepped toward the front of the table to close off his approach to Linda. He held up a hand.

"Hey, guys, I'm not here for trouble. I just want to talk business."

"Talk," I said.

"Maybe she doesn't need to hear this," he gestured to a spot at the bar near Carl Marchek.

"Not exactly a private corner," I said, stating the obvious.

"I'm not worried," he said

We took spots at the bar, as I made sure he was as close as possible to the Fed.

"Here's the bottom line, Walker," he said, getting right to it, "our mutual friend was helping us with a deal that went sour on us."

"Listen, I didn't know anything..."

"It doesn't matter. I've convinced my associates that losing the occasional shipment is an occupational hazard. The ongoing cost of doing business. None of our people were seriously hurt and that's the important thing for us."

"So why are you hounding us?"

"I know our approach can be... dramatic at times, but the girl was sort of a key person in our enterprise and was the only person who knew the key contacts in the venture. We think you, or Missy over there, are will be hearing from these other people.

Perhaps you already have. We just want you to pass them on to us."

"What if I just don't approve of your... enterprise, or think I'll be a lot happier just staying out of it?"

"That would be a reasonable choice, but you might want to keep in mind that both my people and these other characters are pretty dangerous and might be willing to go to great lengths to ensure your cooperation... or your silence."

"What if I just go to the police?"

"As far as we're concerned, the cops already have us in their cross-hairs, so what's another rumor. Especially from someone with a relatively short life span."

"What if no one approaches me?"

"Then they'll probably approach the girl. Do her a favor and advise her to cooperate. We tried to have a friendly chat, but the authorities interrupted."

I looked at him pretty closely, but he seemed fairly serious.

"You know, that idea of a 'friendly chat' might hold water a bit better if it hadn't been for the stunt you pulled at Jessie's funeral."

He shook his head sadly.

"That was bad. Disrespectful, and a bit over the top. I had a few philosophical issues with the whole idea, but I had to go with the community. We decided to support Pig Iron, even though he went a bit off the deep end when the girl died. They had a sort of rare spiritual connection. They were, I don't know... symbiotic... anyway, we went along for the ride with him."

"Philosophical issues?"

"I know, I don't really talk like a stereotypical biker. Philosophy was my major at Ohio U. I got my bachelor's and became one of the corporate execu-drones. I even started an ulcer. Then I said the hell with it and joined the world's last free society."

I didn't argue, but I did wonder about the freedom of society that has you disrupting a funeral against your own beliefs.

"OK, just hypothetically," I heard Marchek cough back a chuckle, "let's say I am willing to set up the next deal for you. How do I reach you?"

He handed me a card with no names, just a couple of phone numbers on it, then stood up to leave.

"Do you mind if I ask a philosophical, none-of-my-business question."

"Sure," he answered.

"The last deal went bad. Why should this one go any better?"

He gave me an odd smile.

"Good old fashioned American optimism. Besides, the last time they took us by surprise. We'll be better prepared this time."

It made sense that another attempt to do Jessie's deal might flush out the crowd that hijacked the deal last time. Maybe it was worth keeping an eye on it to see if it also flushed out Jessie's killer.

"What do you mean, keep her?" Dave asked

"Don't I have a say?" Linda squawked.

"Look, Dave, she's as safe here as anywhere else and at least some of the people might not even think to look for her here. It's a good place to keep her under wraps."

"But what about those motorcycle psychos?"

"Well, they don't seem to have a lot of trouble there, either. They've just threatened us, so you have to figure they'll wait a bit before they come after us again."

"What about work?"

"What were you doing about work when you were at my place?"

"I know, but it's about time for me to go back."

"OK, we can do it like that, I suppose... have you keep moving and never stay in the same place twice. I still think you would be better off here for the weekend."

"Well, well, maybe you have other plans for the weekend, Brad Walker?"

"I have a couple of friends coming in from Ft. Wayne..."

"So you're spending the weekend with that Casey chick?"

"Yeah, why? You're supposed to be hiding out, but I suppose you can come with us."

"Sure. Be a big fucking third wheel and do what?"

"Oh, I don't know... keep me company... hold my hand?"

"Go fuck yourself." She grumbled.

"Those weren't our stakes," I said, grinning.

That brought a laugh in spite of herself.

"Listen, you can come back if you insist, but I just think you'll be safer here."

"Do I get to object?" Dave asked.

"No." I answered.

"Seriously, if she comes across your mom, she's liable to draw Linda here into the 'get Jeff Chandler married' conspiracy."

"Ooh," Linda answered. "Maybe you're right, maybe I should stay here and meet your mother."

I started to respond, but Dave began laughing. "It's a condition of her bail. She has to remain in the jurisdiction. We just decided to give you a hard time."

I was doing about 70 mph, heading north on I-75 coming up on the Marathon Oil refinery. The refinery was a distinctive landmark, with one of its round storage tanks painted to resemble a baseball to advertise their sponsorship of Tiger games on WJR. The road curves to the right as it rises to an elevation of 25-30 feet. Just then, my left front tire blew. I struggled to control the car around the curve in something like a straight path. I don't remember doing much of any of it, but I got off the gas, flipped on my turn signal, and eased the Cutlass onto the shoulder of the road. I did see a circular hole appear in the windshield with a spiderweb of tiny cracks surrounding it. When I got the car to the side of the road I dove under the dashboard as a few more shots cracked the windshield. Whoever it was had shot my tire and was now trying to punch a few holes in me.

I saw a red flashing light washing over the car and then a searchlight hit the car. "Hey, that was pretty good driving... you OK, Walker?"

Talbert, my faithful shadow, saw me pull to the side of the road with an apparent flat, but I wasn't sure he realized there was a sniper out there

"Yeah, put out that light! There's a sniper. He might still be..." I heard the gun report over the sound of traffic. "...out there, shooting."

The light had stopped moving and I heard nothing. "Talbert?" I called. I thought I heard a groan in answer.

I was torn between wanting to help and knowing I was better off hunkered down. The first problem, though was the lights.

The searchlight still set on the front of the car and the red flasher was still going as well. The second thing was the position of the cars. Talbert had come alongside leaving no room between us to slip out, and I had, more or less, pinned myself against the guardrail.

I killed my car lights, prompting more shots through the windshield.

The back window on the opposite side of the car was the darkest corner available for me to try to escape. I had to be careful because it was a long way down if I didn't land inside the guardrail. I gathered myself and vaulted over into the back seat. I landed head down, feet in the air, hardly an Olympic effort, struggling to pull my head out of the foot well, feeling briefly like an overturned turtle. However, on the good side, no gunshots.

As I cautiously was rolling down the rear window I heard a different sort of shot, more a boom than a crack. I waited a second before crawling out head first. As I circled behind the cars, I saw a human figure crouched behind the Ford.

"Talbert?"

"Still in the car," the figure replied

"Who are you?"

"A friend. You OK, Walker?."

OK? Try scared shitless.

"Well, I'm not injured."

"I'll cover you to get in and kill his lights."

"I don't... "

Listen, I can cover you, or you can cover me. I think I know where the sniper's set up, but..."

"OK, I'll go. Don't rush me."

"I'll get the searchlight," he said blasting it with his gun.

Creeping behind the gunman, I worked around to the door and eased it open. I pulled the flashing light's power cord from his cigar lighter and killed the headlights. "You OK, Talbert?" This time he groaned for sure. I picked up the radio mic.

"This is an emergency. We're under fire on north I-75 near the Marathon Oil refinery. There is an officer shot... repeat, an officer shot..."

THIRTY—FOUR
Jeff Chandler's Night Out

Take the time to journey to the center of the
mind
   Journey to the Center of the Mind,
       —The Amboy Dukes

"He pulled up to see if I was OK, and they shot him."
"Who are they?"
"Whoever shot at me."
"And who was that?"
"Some bastard with a rifle," I answered.
"How do you know Sgt. Talbert?"
"He's investigating the death of a friend of mine."
"Who's that?"
"A woman named Jessie Royce."
"The girl in the river?"
"Yes."
*"Did Sgt. Talbert suspect you in the girl's
death?"*
"I don't know... ask him!"
*"Do you have any idea about who might be
shooting at you?"*
"Hell, no."
*Is there anybody who might want to see you
dead?*
Christ, where do I start?
"No idea," I lied, with conviction.

I spent about five hours that Friday night into Saturday
morning answering those same questions, sometimes a friendly
chat, sometimes a serious interrogation, but a constant loop, like
the 8-track player in my ventilated Olds 442.
  Talbert had lost a lot of blood, but was going to survive, they
told me. I have to admit I had a bit of mixed feelings about that.

Somehow I knew he was going to blame me for somebody else shooting him.

By the time the cavalry had arrived, my "friend" had disappeared into the darkness and the cops really wanted to pin the whole thing on me, but fortunately, Michigan apparently had not had the foresight to pass a law making it illegal to be shot at, so they eventually kicked me loose.

My 442, without windshield, was still drivable on the spare, so I limped it back home, not even wanting to start inquiring if Allstate Insurance actually covered bullet holes. The border guard was one I was familiar with. He just looked warily at the car, then waved me through, not saying anything, thank God.

I got a few hours nap, showered, changed, and borrowed Mac's '67 Camaro. I cruised out to Grosse Pointe Woods, getting to Casey's just a little after fashionably late.

"Glad you could make it... Brad," Casey said with a phony smile. I smiled back. Even when I was the target, I always loved when she was being sarcastic.

"I had a bit of car trouble." I said, noncommittally.

"Car trouble, my ass," Mark chuckled, "he probably had a better offer. What happened, Chandler, couldn't kick her out of bed?"

Mark Brandon had been a salesman at the station Casey and I worked at in Fort Wayne. He and his wife Carol had been good friends of Casey while she was married and had known we were seeing each other before her divorce. We used to do dinner and dancing and bowling and all the usual foursome stuff.

"Well, I'm just glad to see you, big guy," Carol said giving me a big hug and kiss. "You're looking good, Jeff..."

I suspected a punch line and I got it:

"...or do we all have to call you Brad, now?"

"Call me anything you want, baby, just call me."

We all chuckled

I was feeling great, nothing like old friends and good memories to provide a break from the life or death sword that seemed to be hanging over me for the moment.

After some conversation and updates, the girls were getting dressed for dinner and, of course, the guys were simply waiting for the women.

As I had speculated, Bobby, the kid dating the girl next door, showed up in a Lincoln limousine. Eddie, the ex-fighter, got out from the driver's seat.

Bobby smiled crookedly. "Hey guys," he said. "Why don't you take the limo if you're going out. It's paid for the night anyway, and Eddie would probably rather drive than sit."

Mark and I looked at each other and shrugged, then I saw a slow smile cross his face.

"Sure if it's OK with you," I said to the driver

"Sure, glad to take you anywhere you want to go Mr… Walker."

I introduced Eddie to Mark, who was fascinated by Eddie's previous profession. "I hear you were a fighter, Eddie?" Mark asked.

"Yeah, I fought light heavy mostly, though I had a few middleweight bouts as a kid."

"Were you any good?"

"Nah. Good at getting hit. I was tough and would go the distance… you know, give the guy a workout, but I really didn't win a lot," He shrugged. "What else, huh? I wasn't no good at anything else. All I could ever do was fight."

"You ever fight anyone famous?"

"Joe Walcott."

The name meant nothing to me, but Mark was very impressed. "Jersey Joe Walcott? Wow!"

"Fifth round, as I remember. Don't think I even saw the punch coming. I did spar with Sugar Ray."

"Really?" You didn't have to be a boxing fan to know who Sugar Ray Robinson was.

"He used to spar with bigger guys sometimes, you know, to build his strength. He had fast hands like you'd never believe. It was like fighting lightning. Only one other guy I ever saw with hands that fast… Bobby Charlton."

"Charlton? Really?"

"I figured you met him, since he was friends with Joe's sister."

"Jessie? I didn't know she knew Charlton. You say they used to go out together?"

"Well, not talkin' out of turn, I saw them together over at that juke joint at 20 Grand and once down at the Rooster Tail. All this before I knew she was Joe's sister."

"So they weren't still seeing each other?"

He shrugged like a man who had a lot of practice at it. I understood. In his profession, it didn't do to be too curious or too talkative.

"You and Joe still trying to find out who killed her, or are you leaving it for the cops to handle?"

"We're still looking, even if we're not making much progress."

"I know Mr. Donovan and his boss are very interested in finding out who killed her, too."

Mark started to ask a question, but I gave him a very subtle shake of the head to forestall him.

I changed the subject.

"I had no idea Charlton was a boxer."

"Oh, he was a great young welterweight until he lost a couple of fingers in an accident. Only we know it wasn't exactly an accident"

We smiled at each other while Mark gave me another quizzical look.

"Joe tells me you live across the river over in Windsor,"

"Yeah, you do a lot of driving over there?"

"I used to go over there all the time with Mr. Donovan. He sort of owns the company, so he gets to use the cars all the time, I think he had a girl over there for a while… but then he bought his own car beginning of this year and so I don't get over much any more. Great town, though."

The girls seemed to be less impressed than we thought about our plan when they finally came out.

"We're taking a limo?" Casey asked with a real note of skepticism.

"Sure, why not?" I answered.

She looked at me, then Eddie, then back toward the house, then, calculations over, she smiled at me. She had figured out it was a free deal.

"So where to, folks?" Eddie was consummately professional as he opened the doors.

"Oh, I don't know… I think I've heard of a place called the Red Fox."

Eddie smiled at me. "Oh, I think I've been there a few times," he said with a wink. "I'm sure can find it."

The *Red Fox* was a popular location, in spite of, or more likely because of it being a widely know mob hangout. On any given day, you could find politicians, labor leaders, local celebrities, and racketeers all sitting down for drinks and dinner at the Red Fox. In fact, only a few years later it would have its most famous claim to fame as the last place Teamsters' boss Jimmy Hoffa was seen alive.

In spite of our stylish arrival, we found ourselves sitting at the bar waiting for a table, and trying to talk ourselves into a drink.

"But I'm 25 years old! I have two kids."

"I'm sorry, ma'am, we have to see ID."

"Well, that's just ridiculous," Carol, who also didn't have her license with her, chimed in.

"Rules are rules," Mark argued sagely, having collected his beer already, "they must have found out how silly you two get when you get a few drinks in you."

Casey wrinkled her nose in annoyance. "Oh, Mark... you're just so *funny*."

"Fine," she said to the bartender. "I'll have a Coke."

I bit my lip to keep from chuckling.

"Ginger Ale," Carol said with a curled lip like a kid about to take Castor oil.

Just then, Matt Donovan, the Mob boss' right hand man, saw me and walked over.

"Hey Walker... I heard about that thing last night... are you OK?"

"What thing last night?" Casey asked.

"You mean he didn't tell you? Some lunatic was shooting cars out on I-75. He put several holes in Brad's convertible, shot an off duty cop, and in general created major chaos."

"Car trouble! Car Trouble?" Casey sputtered. Somebody tries to kill you and..."

"Whoa, whoa... it's just like he said, a lunatic taking potshots at cars, nobody's after me, honest."

Casey looked toward me inquisitively. I shrugged in response. I couldn't be sure I wasn't the target, but I was at a complete loss to explain how someone knew when I was coming and could pick my car out of a crowd on a highway in the dark.

THIRTY—FIVE
Dangerous Men

I'm in with the 'in' crowd, I know where the
in crowd goes...
                    —*The "In" crowd*, Dobie Gray

I hadn't exactly wanted to tell the whole story, in part because even I was having trouble believing the whole thing, but Donovan's comment forced me into giving at least a short version of last night's events. I did remind myself of the one question nagging at me about the whole thing. The sniper.

To hit a moving car at night had to require a shooter with pretty good skill, possibly somebody with a military background? I thought about the mysterious "Mr. Rice" and his bad leg. But the big question was... how could anybody know *where* to find me.

I didn't talk about my mysterious 'friend' either, but he had to somehow be accounted for, as well. If he knew about the attack, why help me? And, if he was following me, who put him on my tail?

"Can your friends spare you a couple of minutes, Brad? I have a couple of people I'd like you to meet."

"Sure, no problem," I answered. "Sorry, kids, it's the price of fame and sex appeal." My friends responded with raspberries and catcalls.

We walked over to his table, where two middle aged men sat in front of beers.

They were Walter Rizzo from Kansas City and Joe Pantaro of New York... we did a quick round of 'glad to meet you'.

"Look, I just wanted you to know that nobody we know had any involvement or knowledge of your shooting last night.

Sure and he'd tell you if they did.

"OK," I said, hoping I didn't sound too skeptical, "but I think I can use your help."

Donovan raised an eyebrow. I explained about what I had been thinking about the difficulty of shooting a car at night.

"I figure your organization might know some of the people who might be capable of that kind of trick shooting and we could see if the folks who sent him are involved in Jessie's death."

"I don't know. You have to understand Vietnam is turning out a whole new crop of trained snipers, a lot of them with night shooting experience... not to mention new specialized stuff to see night targets better."

"Really?"

"Yeah, the government is trying to keep a lid on the stuff, but some of that gear is trickling through the net. You're sure this isn't just coincidence?"

"Hell, I'm not sure of anything. It's just hard to believe in random chance."

"And you've got a line on who killed the girl?"

"No, I just think someone out there thinks I do."

"Maybe you do know something without knowing how it fits in."

I shrugged. He was right, of course, but how to figure out what it might be?

When I got back to the gang, our mob connection seemed to have paid off. We had an excellent table, the girls got their beverages and there was a table of various appetizers, complements of the management.

Casey had apparently filled Mark and Carol in on the entire set up with me, our previous meeting with Donovan, the drug lords, and the mob all tangled together.

I could tell they were all worried. So I rejoined the table with a little humor.

"Don't worry guys, they promised not to shoot me until after dessert."

"Oh, yeah, that's funny," Casey grumbled.

"No, seriously guys, these people don't scare me nearly as much as a few others I've run across."

"Jeff, can't you go to the police, explain the situation..." Carol suggested.

"And tell them what? That the mob asked me a couple of questions? That several criminal organizations think I'm the key to a drug smuggling operation? If they believe me, they'll lock me up as a drug smuggler. If they don't, they'll end up giving me one of those fancy jackets with no pockets."

"OK," Mark said, "what can we do to help?"

"Stay out of it. It's bad enough for me to have to try to figure my own way out without having to worry about danger to my friends. If they get me, then maybe the cops can have them. But until we can prove they've done something, there isn't much we can do.

"Jeff..." Casey began

"Enough of this," I declared. "We'll eat dinner. If the food isn't poisoned, then we'll worry about what to do tomorrow."

"How did you meet this girl anyway?" Carol asked.

"Well, a long time ago, far, far away, there was a place called the Dearborn Stag House..."

Dinner arrived while Casey was telling the Brandons about how she loved her new job as a Montessori pre-school teacher, and of having her girls' tuition paid as a benefit. As I started in on my steak, Mitchell Martin walked up to the table. He stood for a moment looking malevolent, then walked away.

"Creepy," Carol said.

"OK, now *he's* scary. What was that about?" Mark asked.

"I think he was debating whether or not it was good to see I was still OK." I said. "The cop that got shot was a friend of his."

"Well, it isn't your fault, you didn't shoot him."

"Yeah, but that's sort of why he's an *ex*-cop. Little details like innocence never bothered him."

Just as we got up from the table, Donovan returned.

"Hey, guys, It's a beautiful night, and I was thinking of taking a little late night cruise on the river. Thought maybe you and your friends might want to come along?"

I tried to beg off, late night last night, need to get home to free the baby sitter... but he was pretty insistent.

"OK. How about tomorrow? No excuses. It's supposed to be a great day. You and your friends as my guest."

I was still hesitant about the river, having trouble looking at it, or thinking about it.

"Sure," Mark said. "It really sounds like fun."

There. I was going, anyway.

"Bayview Yacht Club, say about 11:30... Noon?"

"OK, we'll be there."

THIRTY–SIX
Cruisin'

11:45 at the big 8, Steve Williams with you on a sunny Sunday. And wouldn't you just love to be out on the Detroit River, cruising? Here's the next best thing Frankie Ford and 'Sea Cruise.' (song)

Sunday morning Mark insisted on driving, so the four of us piled into the Brandons' brand new Buick Skylark and followed the river down to Bayview Yacht Club.

"I grew up on the water," Mark said, cheerily. "Over in Grand Haven, on Lake Michigan. We sailed everything from little dinghies all the way to lake racing yachts. This Donovan got a power cruiser, or does he sail?"

I shrugged. "I guess it's a power boat."

"We'll find out in a few minutes," Carol said. "I swear sometimes he's such a child."

Donovan's boat was a 31-foot Chris Craft Commander.

"Very nice" Mark said. "Must have set you back a good chunk."

"Oh yeah, but it's great," Donovan said. "I can go out cruising any time I want. Fish, drink beer, or just watch the water. Cabins below if you or your friends (said with great innuendo) want to spend the night with the water gently rocking. Plus cross the border anytime you want, avoiding the traffic."

"You mean you can just go to Windsor?" Carol asked.

"Sure. All we have to do is check in with the border authorities when we get there."

That's why he stopped taking the limo across the border. He just crossed by boat.

"I do it all the time."

"Process just as easy coming back?" I asked.

"Sure, more questions if you spend the night, and sometimes they look the boat over—just like if you were in a car."

We cast off, and he gave the boat a little throttle as we headed away from the docks. No wake, just like the sign said.

"So what do you folks want to do? I've got skis."

I looked down into the murky water and shook my head energetically.

"The river is muddy, but not as foul as you might think," he said. "Some people actually enjoy swimming and skiing. There are a few beaches up on Lake St. Clair, if you're interested.

"Oh, by the way, there's a bar down in the cabin, it might be too early for you folks, but I'd love a Bourbon with Coke."

"Sure," Carol said, "we were going to change into swim suits and soak up the rays. Beer for you guys?"

"Sure, thanks Carol."

Hey, I know this great spot for just lazing around down south, just off of Grosse Ile. Cool, tree-lined, a perfect place to just relax... what do you say?"

"Hey, you're the Captain." I answered for us all.

He throttled up and began following the river's course southwest toward the center of Detroit.

The girls came out of the cabin delivered the drinks and draped themselves on the benches at the rear, excuse me, stern of the boat.

"So any further thoughts about your investigation?"

"Well, we definitely have drugs as the question. We've got Jessie tied to a bunch of bikers called the Paladins plus, she had ties to Bobby Charlton..."

"Oh, bullshit!" Donovan declared.

I was really surprised by his vehement response.

"I don't think she'd give the time of day to that jigaboo. Now you probably heard that from Charlton or one of his four aces, right? If you listen to that little 3-fingered spook, he's bedded almost every woman in metro Detroit."

I shrugged. "Listen, my guy just saw them dancing or talking on several occasions. Nobody said she was banging him." *Although with Jessie...*

"Oh," he said, looking less aggravated.

"On the other hand, somebody killed Charlton and put him in Jessie's car. That's got to be personal, don't you think?"

Donovan nodded. "So what about Friday's shooting? Do you think the spooks are blaming you for Charlton's death?"

"Well, that was the killer's intention, wasn't it? Charlton thought Jessie had scooped up the money and drugs but when he found the car, he realized that his partner got there ahead of him and got them. So his partner bumped him off."

"Couldn't she have just hid the stuff somewhere else?" he asked.

"Maybe, but apparently Charlton's partner didn't want to share anyway."

"OK, who's his partner."

"No idea."

"Could it be one of his followers?" Mark asked. "I mean, Caesar was done in by Brutus... Kennedy by Johnson..."

He grinned at me, knowing that I would remember one of the sales guys we worked with in Ft. Wayne, who used to bend people's ears unmercifully with his theory that the JFK assassination was a plot orchestrated by the vice president. "It was in Texas, for god's sake!" He always yelled, as if that made the theory more plausible

"Sure. I don't believe it, though, I think it would either require agreement between all four of his guys, or it would inevitably lead to an internal power struggle."

"But if one could convince the others that Charlton bought it from someone else... you for example..."

"Never work," I explained, "they've met me. They know I'm not really the violent type. Whoever shot him in the head had to be someone he knew and trusted."

"Or perhaps a woman," Mark suggested, nonchalantly.

"Well, it's likely his partner in the deal was on *that* side," I said, gesturing toward downtown Windsor on our left. "Why couldn't it be a woman?"

"A woman!" Donovan sputtered, "It couldn't happen. You've got drug smugglers, mobsters, hit men, cops... serious men, trained killers. How could a woman be tough enough to gain their respect? These are old fashioned guys who expect women to be wives or mistresses. There's no danger of womens' lib in our business."

"No, she would be more subtle. She would suggest instead of order, cajole instead of command. She wouldn't try to out

tough them, she'd play to weakness and frailty. Encourage them
to be more protective of her."

Even jealous.

"I mean take a look at how Jessie managed to set up this
drug deal, it wouldn't be that hard…"

"No. Maybe you're right." Donovan said.

"Most likely," I suggested, "a woman would seduce one
guy… who would then front for her."

"But wouldn't we have seen this woman in the picture?"
Mark asked.

"You'd think so, but I don't know a lot about the Canadian
end of the operation."

"Well, I do," Donovan noted, "and the closest thing they
have to a woman is a couple of those fruity little French guys.

"Besides, wouldn't the body in the car point toward a guy? I
mean that body dump might represent a good revenge if the girl
was still alive, but I don't see that personal motive working for a
woman."

I nodded. "It would probably take a guy to bundle Charlton
into the trunk of the car as well, I suppose."

"So, you go out every weekend?"

"Oh, hell, not just weekends, I'm out as long as the weather
is warm. I even occasionally loan it out to a few of my friends—
Mitch Martin, Mike Lang… I even rented it once to one of
Charlton's boys, the one they call Mark, I think. Him and that
boxer kid, Ray-Ray. They paid me 500 bucks. I have to admit I
didn't even know those people went in for that sort of thing.
Who ever heard of niggers boating? But then I did see the girls
they took out and I wouldn't mind being stuck in the dark, if you
know what I mean?"

We cruised on down past the city and the river turned
southward, I could feel myself beginning to relax to the hum of
the engine, not to mention a couple of beers and began for the
first time in a while to begin to enjoy myself.

As we reached the island, we could see the spot he
described. The trees lining the shores dappled the sunlight, so
the shade kept a cool breeze along the water and kept the
shimmering water dancing. The Canadian fort at Amherstburg
stood almost as a guardian of the shoreline.

Donovan opened a cabinet and pulled out the anchor.

"Hey," Mark said, "what kind of rope is that?"

"Oh, yeah," Donovan said. "It's nylon. It's only a fraction of the weight of the regular hemp ropes. I picked it up a month or so back. One of my buddies lost the old one. I don't know if he just flunked knot tying or he got it caught in the prop of another boat.

Caught in a prop my ass. I think the rope and anchor were used to get rid of a friend of mine.

"Did he at least pay for the new gear?" I asked, still trying to keep the light mood.

"He hasn't yet, but I know Mike's good for it. I just hope he doesn't pay it in that Canadian funny money. It just doesn't look right, does it? Oh. What am I saying? That's what they pay you, don't they, Brad?"

"Yeah," Mark added, "do they give you crayons to color that stuff in, or do they do it for you?"

I chuckled along, realizing that for the first time, since Charlton's death, "Inspector Walker" had a prime suspect, Michael Lang, but what was I supposed to do with him?

THIRTY—SEVEN
Meeting of the minds

I didn't have long to mull over the question when I got back to the apartment and found Sgt. McGowan and Carl Marchek waiting for me.

"Jesus Christ, Walker, you're one cool son of a bitch. People try to kill you off, and you just run off for a weekend of fun and (I hope) wild sex." Marchek said.

"We would have put out an alert," McGowan said, but your friend McCarthy told us where you went and when you'd be back."

"Any idea who shot at me?"

"No, but they found the sniper's perch," the Mountie said. "He had taken a spot at the top of one of the refinery's cracking towers."

"So he probably had been up there before?"

Marchek nodded. "Detroit police aren't completely witless, they're checking the refinery workers and people caught trespassing on the grounds."

"So, Walker, any speculation about who might have been up there?"

"That was my next question for you guys. But I do think I might have a suspect and an idea worth checking out."

I told them what I had learned on the afternoon's cruise. No names, of course, except for Michael Lang.

"It's all a bit thin, isn't it?" McGowan asked. "I mean it could just be a slipped knot as easily as anything else."

"Maybe, but the coincidence is astronomical," I answered. A boat turns out to lose an anchor at just about the same time as a girl ends up dropped in the river. It seems at least worth asking who had boats or access to a boat to dispose of her."

"OK, we'll check that out. Any other ideas?"

"Well, our bikers gave me an idea," I told Marchek. "This thing started with a drug deal gone bad... so, maybe we should recreate the original conditions. If our killer hijacks the deal again, we've got a shot to catch him, if the deal goes down, we'll at least have all the known suspects in one place."

"Who's going to be the point guy on this one? The girl's dead."

"Well, I seem to know all the players and the bikers seem to have already nominated me as the man in the middle, so, I guess I'm *it*."

"You? what do you know about facilitating a drug deal?"

"Nothing, but then Jessie probably didn't have any experience, either. The smugglers need to know what they're doing, all I am is the messenger."

"Who's going to be in on this deal?" Marchek asked.

"Why even ask questions like that, you know I couldn't answer them. What I need to know is if you guys can have the cavalry ready when the whole thing goes down or goes sour."

They both stared at me for a minute, then shrugged.

"OK, I can see you arranging the deal, but how do you know for sure this one will go bad?"

I don't know for sure, but everybody still has the same motives so you have to expect a similar attempt.

"What makes you so certain you can get the hijackers to show up?" McGowan asked.

"I think I'm going to end up inviting them. I'm going to talk to all of my suspects and set it up. The hijackers will be there because somebody invited them last time, and I think I know who they are. Besides, there has to be an inside guy, because somebody called for them in the first place.

"The hijackers were a distraction the first time. Somebody involved in the *exchange* did the rip-off."

"The girl," Marchek said.

"Don't think so. Something my source said about not having women in certain roles. Even it she was it, they'll find somebody else this time.

"With more money and dope available, they'll try again. We just need to see who disappears with the goods."

"How do you know it's going to be the same outfit stealing the prize?" Mc Gowan asked.

"Are we going to let them try this thing, or sit around nitpicking it to death?" I grumbled.

In some ways I knew what I knew, in others I couldn't explain, in a few corners I was still doubting my conclusions, but one thing was for sure, and that was what I was counting on.

"This guy got away with it last time, because he was very, very smart. He was meticulous in his plan and even had substitute suspects, people like me, at every turn, in case the cops started nosing around.

"This son of a bitch thinks he's smarter than all of us and is going to try to prove it, again."

THIRTY-EIGHT
Confrontation

It was a dangerous idea, but it was the only one I had to trap the killer. It wasn't so much that I didn't recognize the risk, as it was that there were at least three outfits ready to drop the hammer on me, anyway. Might as well go down swinging.

I called Dave, explaining what I wanted to do and asked him to bring Linda up.

He offered a clear and honest assessment of my plan.

"Have you lost your fucking *mind*?"

"Probably, and I need your help."

There was a long silence, even though we both already knew the answer. "OK," he finally said, "What am I doing?"

"I need your electronic genius. Need you to make a little radio transmitter. 'bout the size of a transistor radio. In fact that's exactly what it should look like."

"Listening device? Why can't you just get one from the Feds. They have better stuff and can make it any size you want."

"Sure, but if the Feds provide the device, I can guarantee that only the Feds will be listening to it. Besides, some of the people I have in mind are kind of allergic to the FBI."

"I think I can put together something, with a receiver, but it won't have a lot of range... couple hundred yards, maybe. What's it about?"

"There's something I don't get about this thing, but if I put our little radio in the right hands, I think we might actually get the proof we need."

"OK, T J, but can you at least let the police handle it from there?"

"Sure, Dave."

"How much time do I have?"

"It's for Wednesday night."

"Nothing like a rush job. Have it for you Tuesday, when we come up."

"Tuesday?"

"I want a day to try to talk you out of this damn foolishness."

Next, I called the Paladins and let them know that I was setting up the deal.

"Wednesday night? That doesn't leave us a lot of time to make our plans."

"It also doesn't give your opposition a lot of time to get ready either."

"You're sure they're going to be there?"

"If they don't know yet, they'll know soon."

My first call for Monday was to our promoter friend, Armand.

"I need to talk to John… you know, your new partner?"

"John? No, no, it's Matthew you're probably looking for. He's Charlton's no. 1 'Gospel' and he's the one who we've been seeing around here. He's the new fellow in charge."

"Fine, tell *him* I need to meet with John."

There was silence for a minute or so.

"Fine," he said as the verbal equivalent of a shrug. "I will pass the message along. Should I tell them what it's about?"

"You don't know. More importantly, Armand, you don't want to know."

I Called Matt Donovan and explained what I was up to and why. He was willing to provide whatever support was necessary.

As I was leaving the studio, my phone rang again.

"Hey, Brad, it's Joe Landis… sorry to bother you at work…"

"No, listen man, any time you want to talk… what's up?"

"You know, I'm just getting around to going through some of Jessie's papers and stuff and her mail, and I found her last paycheck. I finally found out who Jessie was last working for."

"Yeah."

"Some company called WestGrand Productions."

"WestGrand… that little son of a bitch!"

Armand was in the studio recording a jazz quintet. He had turned and was on the verge of speaking when I grabbed him and slammed him across the sound board into the studio window.

"You underhanded son of a bitch," I held him pinned to the board with my forearm tightening his windpipe.

Bennie, who moved pretty quickly for his size, laid his hand on my shoulder, attempting to restrain me. I turned and looked back at him and I heard an angry growl coming from my depths. He obviously saw something in my eyes and decided not to interrupt.

"Brad, what in the hell is wrong with you, my friend..."

I was in no mood for his snake-oil charm. I cut him off with a little pressure.

"I understand Jessie and Linda used to work here?"

"Oh, my god." His face fell. He might have looked even more baleful than he had after I had been worked over in my 'meeting' with Bobby Charlton.

"Listen, it wasn't what you think, Brad."

"Oh, I'll bet it *was,* Armand. The girls were window dressing at the party. They were there on the payroll."

"No, no, it is true the girls did office work for us..."

"'Give them everything they need,' you told that little waitress, didn't you. This was all part of your plan."

"No! It is right that I invited the girls to the party. I thought they would enjoy it. I did... I admit I pointed you out to them, but I never told them to go to you or stay with you."

"Sure, Armand, it was just our charm."

"Brad, I was not trying to buy your cooperation or... procure girls for you like some sort of pimp. I thought it would be nice for the girls to enjoy the event and I sort of thought it would be nice for you to meet them and vice versa.

"They were just invited to the party, they weren't working."

I shook my head angrily.

"Whatever you might think, please do not be hasty in telling our friend Charles. He has taken that girl's death very seriously, and is in great pain. We can't compound his agony by suggesting that the girl held no feelings for him. I fear he might do something desperate."

Charlie? We hadn't spoken much, and I knew he wasn't taking Jessie's death very well. Armand's suggestion that he was in serious despair was certainly something I hadn't noticed.

But I wasn't even sure I could believe him. Even if the girls weren't under orders, or went 'above and beyond'. or if it started as a set up and grew into something bigger. The most amazing night of my life was apparently something this little… *promoted.*

"So the girls never got paid… a little extra?" I asked.

It was a shot in the dark but it hit home. He didn't want to tell me, but it was pretty obvious he couldn't lie out of it either.

"I could just ask Linda?"

"It was just a bonus for the marvelous work they did. Even she would tell you that we paid them before the party and they were under no obligation to come."

True, but then again a boss' invitation to a party does sort of carry its own encouragement.

I sort of wanted to believe him, but I wasn't sure I could believe anything he told me, but if I wasn't at least going to let him explain himself why was I there?

"Please, Brad, I know I have lost some of your trust, but for our friend Charles' sake could you at least not upset him further at this time."

Who the hell knew what I was going to tell Charlie? I thought about what Allan had said about how we didn't talk much these days. How was I going to tell him the girls had been on Armand's payroll?

I realized I had become the center of attention, with the musicians standing at the window marveling at the lunatic trying to kill Armand. I assumed Bennie and Phil, the sound engineer, were standing behind me wondering how to stop it as well.

I also realized I still had the choke hold on him, but I sort of had decided not to actually kill him, but had no idea what to do with him. I dropped him to the floor, then sank angrily into the chair I had hauled him out of.

Bennie reached over and helped Armand to his feet, looking back with a half-smile.

"I think he really did want to tell you, Brad," the usually silent Bennie said, "but, as Caesar said, the dice was cast. He couldn't tell you the girls worked here without you thinking it was a set-up."

It was then that it occurred to me that Armand was another perfect suspect. He had ties to Charlton, Jessie knew a secret he was desperate to keep silent, and, of course, drugs and music are as natural a combination as peanut butter and jelly or mashed potatoes and gravy.

Maybe...

"So tell me, what do you guys know about the drug business?"

Armand's eyes widened in fear for a moment, but I never really got the answer I wanted from him because I could hear the control room door opening behind me.

THIRTY–NINE
The Usual Suspects

"Good Afternoon, Brother Walker,"

The cool, baritone voice came from behind me. John, the new leader of the Charlton gang, had entered the control room.

"I'm glad to see you're feeling fit after your little highway misadventure. Just so you know, your shooter was an overzealous brother who thought you had a hand in Bobby's death. Don't worry, I put the word out. Set it straight."

I blinked at him, a bit slack-jawed if my mouth wasn't completely agape. Not only was it an attempt to kill me, but he's already assuring me there would be no more attempts. Maybe I was wrong about the lack of internal power struggle.

"Who was it?"

"Doesn't matter... I put the word out, you're safe. At least from the soul brothers. Them eye-talians might feel differently."

"The Mob is after me?'

He shrugged. "I just know they've been paying an awful lot of attention to this whole thing. You've picked up a tail, you know, and I am not talking about that stupid cop."

"No idea who it is?"

"Seen the cat before. Maybe with the Canadian mob boss, Ferante, or Mitch Martin..."

Or Michael Lang.

But if my tail and "friend' was working for Lang, why did he go out of his way to save *my* hide?

"Now, if you gentlemen will excuse us," John said to Armand and Bennie. "We have some private business to discuss."

"You seemed pretty certain that I was the Man, what made you so sure it was me and not one of the others?"

"When I was a kid, my Mom made me take religious instruction. I remembered that the gospel of John was the only one actually written by a true apostle. There was also that whole last will be first and first last thing."

He nodded.

"I suppose you're using Matthew around here as a front?"

"Well, the confusion is an advantage, but the truth is each of us have particular interests and he's the one most excited by music. Luke handles our real estate."

"Real estate?"

"Sure, we don't intend to be in the powder business for the rest of our lives. Hoping to retire by 30."

I smiled. Had to keep in mind this guy was very smart.

"I was hoping your organization might be willing to help me with a little project. After all, it was you guys who provided the diversion while Jessie and her partners ripped off that drug deal, right?"

He looked at me for a second. Then nodded.

"It was all a put up," I said. "You were supposed to make noise and scatter everybody, then get which: the money, or the drugs?"

A smile slowly crossed his face.

"Yeah, you read that pretty good. I'm not sure exactly how it worked, but we got paid up front on the deal. We were supposed to show up and make a lot of noise, scattering everybody, then afterward we were supposed to also get the drugs to sell to our usual partners."

"Mr. F."

"Best not to use names."

"But it's worth making sure we're all not using the *same* name to avoid confusion."

He nodded.

"But what I don't get is: Weren't the Canadians putting up the money for this deal in the first place?"

"I thought so, too, but apparently there was a new money source on that side."

"This still doesn't make sense," I argued. "This was, I would assume, a fairly small scale deal. A test run. Why wouldn't they wait until they started moving bigger quantities? Wouldn't the best thing have been to wait until they were moving 'big weight'-isn't that the term-then spring the trap and rip them off?"

"I thought the same thing, until I realized it's more likely a protection racket." He said.

"For a small fee we can insure safe transactions, or more accurately, if you don't' pay…"

"Yeah, Bobby once said he had a man at both ends of the deal."

"And the girl in the middle."

"The girl, yeah, she was a stone gas. That's the dirtiest part. The rest of us already knew and assumed the risks, she was a one time shot—just helping out a friend."

"Which friend?"

"Don't know. She just said helping a friend."

I nodded. Could be a lot of people, Charlton, Armand, Royce, Charlie, Linda, hell even her brother Joe, plus several others…

As I thought about the scheme, another question occurred to me.

"So they paid you guys cash up front as well as the drugs? Doesn't it make you wonder exactly how much your silent partner hoped to make on the back end."

Silent partner… Bennie had the same reasons to be involved as Armand and could have easily tossed a *couple* of Jessies with anchors overboard.

John nodded. "There is something we're missing, but if we knew what it was…"

"Exactly, but I have an idea that might get all of us some answers. After all, you and I have at least one goal in common… who killed our friends. We're most likely both looking for the same guy."

"Sure, but you're probably looking toward the cops, aren't you? All those courts and lawyers…"

"While you had a more biblical style of justice in mind? Either way, we have to catch him, and if he slips past the courts, he's already been tagged."

"So what's your plan?"

"We're going to do the same deal Jessie set up, this Wednesday night."

"Do it again? What you been smokin'? Them honky bikers ain't going to try that again."

"Actually, it's sort of their idea. I think they're itching for a rematch."

He laughed.

"Last time, we had the element of surprise going for us, no one on either side was supposed to get hurt, and we all got paid in advance. This time we're expecting a dangerous shootout and are getting..."

"Absolutely nothing."

"Nothing," he echoed. "So tell me why should we get involved this time?"

I looked him squarely in the eye and said, deadpan, "You shouldn't."

We smiled together in understanding.

I think that's what I like about you, Walker, you're what our Jewish brothers would call *meshugge*... crazy."

"Can't argue with that."

Mitchell Martin had a small office in the Fisher Building.

"You've got a hell of a nerve coming here," he said. "You must think you've got brass ones the size of bowling balls."

"Yeah, who knew?" I said with a half grin. "I just thought I should drop by with the latest news."

I told him about the plan I was working on.

"Why are you telling me? I'm not in the cocaine trade."

"I know, but for reasons I'm not sure I can explain, I trust you. I need you to make sure our mutual friend across the river knows what we're up to."

"What do I look like, Western Union? He's got people... tell them."

"I will, I just don't want any details lost in the translation."

"You're saying somebody in his organization can't be trusted?"

"I'm saying that his right hand man is sort of on the suspect list."

He looked at me with a steely gaze.

"Am I on your suspect list?"

"Yes, but near the bottom." *Why lie?*

"What?"

"Well, you're clearly capable enough, but if you were trying to get information out of the girl, as our killer probably wanted, she'd be missing fingers, not a foot."

Martin did something I didn't think him capable of... he laughed.

"That's pretty good thinking, you'd have made a good cop. But what if the girl was an accident and I *am* your killer."

"Then," I said, "I'll see you Wednesday night."

FORTY

A Little Import Duty

After my Detroit meetings, I came back across the bridge, stopped at an Esso station on Huron Church Rd. for a map of Essex County, and cruised westward along the river looking for a suitable landing spot for our drug flotilla. I decided that down in the boondocks might have some advantage over the city location I suspected Jessie or her 'friend' had chosen. By selecting a location a bit farther downriver, our bikers could put in somewhere south of Detroit like Monroe or Toledo Beach (yeah, it's in Michigan, go figure), and could use Grosse Ile for cover if things got a bit hairy. I found a couple of reasonable locations, then headed back home.

When I got to the apartment, Charlie was sprawled on the couch.

"He got here about 7:00, falling down drunk," Mac said. "He said he needed to talk to you."

"About?"

"Who knows?. He came in saying he had to talk to you, then he curled up and went to sleep. I got a big pizza from Sam's, figuring you guys would probably help me finish it off."

"Well, that was a good idea." Particularly since I was just realizing I hadn't had anything substantial all day.

"You going to wake him up?"

"Nah, let him sleep… for a while anyway."

He smiled. "Anyway, I've got places to be."

"Isn't it a bit late to just be going out?"

"What can I say? Don't wait up, Mom. See you at work."

"Night, Mac."

I ate a couple of slices of the pizza before Charlie stirred.

"Brad?"

"Hey, Charlie."

"Jessie told me what you were doing."

"Jessie?"

"Jessie? Christ... *Linda*... she said you were getting involved in the same ass-out scheme that got Jessie killed! You can't do this... I mean, these are dangerous people. You can get killed."

It sounded pretty serious for Charlie. I looked at him a little more carefully. His usual happy-go-lucky style seemed to have been replaced by a weary, sort of pained, expression. He was tired and genuinely worried.

Armand was right. Charlie was a lot more devastated by Jessie's death than I had imagined.

"I should be the one doing this."

I shook my head, but before I could answer, he continued.

"Listen, Brad, when Jess died, I was furious. Blamed you for getting her into this mess, for not protecting her, for...

"Anyway it was maybe a day or two later when I realized I was insane. If she was choosing to be with you, that was her business. We never made any claims on each other. I knew you well enough to know you wouldn't have gotten her into this drug business. I know you wouldn't have left her holding the bag like that other worthless son of a bitch must've.

"I want that bastard as much as you do. I should be the one out there wearing the bull's eye."

"Won't work, Charlie. I've been wearing the target ever since she popped up in the river. The cops, the crooks, even her crazier than a bedbug mother have all pointed at me already. I'm apparently the last guy to see her, the one she found right after the drug deal went sour. Her most likely confidant. I'm the guy most likely to know the secret that Jessie was killed over. The killer can't take a chance that I know, or will figure it out."

"C'mon, Brad, you can't just leave me with nothing to do. I mean she was my friend, too..."

"Charlie, I understand why you want in on this, but there isn't much for any of us to do at this point. As for getting killed, I hope to be miles away when the shooting starts and die of old age in my own bed.

He grinned at me.

"What happened to 'Live fast, die young?'"

"I think it's a much cooler idea before it becomes a genuine possibility."

"So there's nothing I can do?"

"Sorry, Charlie."

"Sounds like a commercial," he grumbled. Then broke into his classic grin. It was already an old joke, Charlie the Tuna, but it brought us our first genuine laugh in a while.

"She was a hell of a girl, our Jess," he noted.

"She was at least that," I answered, "but you'd know more about that than I would."

"I hear you found out it was Armand who fixed us up."

I really wish I could have seen my face when he said that.

"You'll catch flies that way." The old Charlie was grinning at me.

"Jess told me. That second day, while we were in the pool. That little peckerhead pointed them at us as sort of a favor."

"Favor?"

"Sure, all those times he'd call and ask us to play a few of his artists in a row because he's 'entertaining the big money', or ask us to swing by the studio and meet 'somebody important' or even appearances like at the Stag House? And so, he'd buy dinner, or get concert tickets like Hendrix back in March, or free drinks like the party. It's all the same thing."

I nodded. He was right. We did things for each other all the time. Instead of thinking of it as a bribe, I could have thought of it like Charlie did, a friend introducing another friend to a girl.

"Yeah, you're probably right, but I am wondering about the set up over there, you know... Armand and drugs."

Charlie's eyes narrowed. "Armand and drugs?" he queried, unconvincingly.

"OK, Charlie, spill it."

"Well," he said over about 10 seconds, "those little boosters I use sometimes... they come from Armand. He's got a little supply of happy stuff for the musicians and a few friends, but he's not in the big import/export like his investors, trust me."

Maybe he was right.

"He's got a bad gambling jones, though." Charlie admitted.

"How bad?"

"He's in, at least a bit, to the loan sharks."

"Hence Bennie, the silent partner?"

"Probably. Could... nah, doesn't make sense. Sharks might break his legs, but how would that involve Jess."

"Well, say he's desperate. He gets Jessie to front for him in a drug deal to get him off the hook. When the deal goes south, they take her out."

"Maybe, but if they leaned on her, wouldn't she have pointed to him and why wouldn't they have gone after him?"

Good point. The more I looked at this thing, the more certain I am that she was killed by her partner, whoever he was.

FORTY-ONE
A Little Import Duty

9:15. Brad Walker at the Big 8 on a sweltering Tuesday, with Rufus Thomas... man, it's a bad day for 'Walking The Dog' (Song)

I was struggling to keep a straight face when Chucklehead stuck his head in the studio door. Station management had installed a direct line to the studio, complete with a flashing red light, to call and complain, or pester the jocks. Fred often annoyed us via "Batphone", but he rarely came in, having enough sense to realize how territorial we are in the studio about unwanted visitors, but this time...

"Where the fuck is Kelly?"

"Morning, Fred. It's after 9. Charlie went home."

"That son of a bitch. He was supposed to stay and drive the contest car this afternoon. I called to remind him and he hung up on me."

"Hung up? Are you sure? I mean you were calling from your car phone, right? Sometimes those mobile phones get interference..."

We had all created 'accidental' cut offs, but Charlie had gone one step further. Peeling the cellophane from a cigarette pack (mine, of course), he had crackled the plastic over the mouthpiece of the phone, and shouted:

"Can't talk now, chief, the studio is on fire!"

Then hung up.

Needless to say, Fred couldn't call back without looking like a sucker who believed the studio really was on fire. He also could never tell the story to any of us without feeling a bit foolish.

The bad news was that I couldn't admit to being a witness, either, without looking like a co-conspirator.

"It wasn't interference," he grumbled.

I tried to shrug nonchalantly, but I think I couldn't quite suppress a grin. I began to think he was coming to the realization that I was in on the trick.

"Charlie seemed to be a bit under the weather," I finally answered. "I suppose I can take the car."

I was meeting with our bikers, but I wasn't expecting any trouble that would endanger the 'vette.

"OK, thanks, Walker." He headed toward the door, but stopped.

"Say, Walker, did they ever find who killed that girl? You know, the one from the party."

"Not yet, but we're getting close."

"I was surprised," he said. "I knew the girl, but nobody seemed to want to ask me any questions. Guess I'm not a suspect."

"Probably not."

"But they suspected *you*."

"Well, they sort of quickly figured the crime required a brilliant mind."

He thought for a second and was about to speak when I held my hand up.

(Jingle) More Music, C-K-L-W.
9:27 in the Motor City with Brad Walker and Sam and
Dave... 'You don't know like I know', and believe me
gang I know! (Music Plays)

"You're implying I'm not smart enough to be the killer?"

I smiled, knowingly, then said, "Thanks for coming in, Fred."

Michael Lang met me at the door of the station. I resisted the urge to attack him, but I doubt if I looked pleased to see him.

"My boss wants to see you." He said tersely

"Well I have to drive the contest car for a couple of hours. Maybe a bit of early dinner—this time at *my* favorite restaurant. Say, 5:30?"

I had arranged to meet the bikers at a small hamburger stand just north of Monroe, sort of half way between Toledo and

Detroit. The bikers had taken spots at the counter. The one we had met was sitting next to what I assumed would be the leader, Pig Iron. I took the stool next to him.

"You Walker?"

I nodded. "You Iron?"

He made a grumbling sound that might have been a chuckle. "Waldo said you were some kind of wise ass."

I looked over his shoulder at his compatriot.

Waldo?

"OK, then, all business." I handed him the map I had marked. "3 am. You have two lights on the front of the boat. Horizontal," I gestured with my hand, "indicates the deal is on. Stacking them vertical means no go.

"On the shore, a single light. Red, if there's a problem or delay. Only four men out of the boat, four from the other group. Only two each for the actual exchange. One of them will be holding a small transistor radio."

"What the hell for?"

"Not like people are going to wear name tags or ID's. It's a way of making certain you're dealing with the right people."

"It's dumb."

I shrugged.

"Why don't *you* confirm them."

"Me? I'm not going to be there. I'm just setting the thing up."

"It's a set-up alright," Pig Iron growled, "we show up and the place is crawling with cops. I don't trust this guy."

"Then don't go."

"Wait, let's not get hasty," Waldo asked. "I'm curious, Walker. Why are you doing this? When we talked before, you didn't have any interest in the deal."

"I have my reasons."

"I still don't trust him." Pig Iron growled

"You shouldn't."

Waldo raised an eyebrow.

"I wouldn't trust him as far as I could throw my bike." He said.

I shrugged again.

"This has something to do with the dead girl, doesn't it?" Waldo argued. "I think Walker here knows something about why she got killed."

"I think her killer was involved in the deal." I said.

"So you're using us as bait?"

"More like a gathering of suspects."

"Suspects? How do we know *you* didn't kill her." Pig Iron argued.

"The same way I know you didn't kill her."

"So you think the killer will be there?" Waldo asked.

"He was there the last time."

"So how are you going to recognize him? Didn't you say you weren't going to be there?"

I smiled enigmatically. "He'll find you, I think."

"Me?"

"One of you, anyway."

"Doesn't matter," Pig Iron grumbled. "We're out of this. I don't trust you."

"Have a nice trip back."

"Wait, wait…" Waldo implored. "Let's just talk about this."

"No. You guys talk about it," I said, heading toward the door. "I give less than a damn whether you do this thing or not."

The Tunnel Bar-B-Que is a Windsor landmark. Since 1941, Gus Racovitis and his family have been feeding folks from both sides of the border with fire-roasted, dry-rubbed ribs served with a spicy and unique sauce that can bring tears to your eyes in both senses of the word.

Ferante dismissed Lang, which did nothing to cool our growing animosity. As I expected, word had clearly gotten to him that he was very high on my suspect list, and he was very annoyed that I was trying to keep him on the edge of this deal.

I ordered the rack of ribs, while our big guy ordered the Two for One chicken and rib combo.

"This is good," he said. "I like this place very much."

"I eat here all the time, you can't get better barbeque on the planet."

"I'm afraid you've been working under a slight misapprehension, here, Walker."

"OK."

"Well, while we did have an interest in the previous deal as a retail distributor, we did not act as the importer in question. Our role was to simply prepare the product for sale and sell it in the usual manner."

"OK, but you have to know who the importer is, don't you?"

"Of course. Michael will be more than willing to take you to them."

Sure, just trust Michael Lang.

"Did you have a financial stake in the last transaction?"

He considered me for a moment.

"They might have borrowed some portion of money from us, but you would have to ask Michael about that."

"Lang handles your money?"

He nodded his head, "I heard you are suspicious of Michael, but he has put our organization on a much more business-like footing. He not only has opened up new revenue possibilities, but he has developed new ways to keep better track of our money.

"It's tricky in an all cash business to keep unscrupulous people from skimming part of the take as it goes through the system. Michael has developed ways of tracing money and has seriously put a dent in our internal losses." *Internal losses?*

"I trust Michael completely and you should, too."

"I'm afraid in my current position I cannot trust anyone completely."

He nodded in understanding.

"On a slightly different subject," I continued, "what do you know about WestGrand Productions?"

"Due to the snowballing gambling debts of your friend, Armand, we own a small percentage of the company. Before you ask, I have no reason to believe he has any interest in competing with us in the import business and I don't think his late partner, Charlton, or his successor, would approve either.

"He does handle a bit of product on a strictly retail level, for his music clients and personal friends, but it was nothing of significance."

"So, you're the folks behind Bennie the silent partner?"

"Well, he corresponds with us, but we have no formal connection with him."

I smiled a bit. But said nothing.

It had become clear it was never formal connections that our killer made use of either. Certainly, through the Canadian organization's link with Bennie, Lang would have had a pipeline to not only Armand, but also Bobby Charlton... and Jessie.

FORTY–TWO

The French revolution?

"I am Marat."

"Just one name, like Elvis… or Superman?"

Michael Lang and the other fellow grinned in response, but our friend Marat was hardly amused.

"It is a *nom de guerre*," he said, dramatically, "to protect our people and to strike fear into the hearts of the *Anglais* who oppress us. He is Danton."

"Marat was a famous French revolutionary," Lang said.

"Wasn't he the one who got knocked off in the bathtub?"

"He was a martyr to the cause of freedom." Marat said.

"Sure." *But he had deadly taste in girlfriends.*

We were meeting in a small restaurant near the Ford Plant, ironically, on Walker Rd. The two French Canadians were the drug buyers.

"We lost the money in the last deal," Danton said, "Why should we try again?"

"Why try in the first place? Everybody I talk to on this deal seems to think there's a guarantee. All I'm doing is pointing you folks at each other and letting nature take its course. You've never seen me. Before or after, know what I mean?"

Danton cocked his head at me.

"There is quick profit in this business," he said.

"And high risk," I answered.

Danton nodded. "Monsieur Lang has been good enough to advance us a portion of the future sale of our product in order to make this second purchase."

"What happens if it doesn't work?"

"We will have to go back to our friends fighting for the freedom of our country. This is why we are uncertain about trying this deal again."

"You asked why we take such risk," Marat said. "We need to raise money, but we cannot do it by conventional means for fear of the authorities learning of our purpose. We are *patriotes* sworn to free our homeland."

"Pardon my ignorance, isn't Canada already a free country?"

"It is free only for the *Anglais*—the English speakers. The English Canada you know has overwhelmed its French people, imprisoned their souls and emasculated their culture. They have driven my countrymen into exile and established dominance over our homeland of Quebec."

"That was a while ago, wasn't it?"

"That's what I tried to tell them," Lang said. "The new Prime Minister of Canada is French, isn't he?"

"Pfah, Trudeau is a lackey! A lapdog to the English power brokers. Nothing will change until we win back our homeland."

"So you need the money for guns?"

"Guns, lawyers, all resources."

I shrugged. "I'm pretty sure I don't want to know too much about your planned revolution."

I then explained the set up for the exchange and the location.

"I do not like this distance from the city."

"Well, last time you were right up here and it all went sideways."

Lang regarded me with surprise.

"How did you know our last location?" he asked.

"I didn't exactly. I just deduced it was nearby from what our friend said."

"You did not say where you would be while this deal is to be done?" Danton asked

"I am going to be home in bed. I have no vested interest in this deal. I am only finishing what my deceased friend started."

Marat glared at me for a minute. "I am not sure I like that you will not be there for the exchange."

"Jessie was there the last time," I pointed out, "and all that guaranteed was that she was killed."

"Keep in mind, the same people who stole your money last time are still out there and will unquestionably try again. I'm not encouraging this thing, just picking a spot for it to happen. Everyone assumes their own risk."

Lang's eyes narrowed, then he nodded.

"Like Walker said, everybody assumes their risk."

"We must think." Danton said.

"Good idea." I answered.

As we approached my car, I noticed someone standing next to it. I looked over at Lang.

"It's OK, Walker. He's with us."

As we got to the car I recognized my 'friend' from the highway.

"His name is Spiros," Lang told me. "The US syndicate asked us to keep an eye on you. I think they meant on this side of the border, but fortunately, Spiros got sort of bored.

"I like your radio station," he said with a grin.

"You get priority on the request line," I said smiling back.

"Thought you'd want to know, it was the cop that set you up for the sniper." Spiros said.

"You're sure."

"Horse's mouth. He set you up for one of Charlton's boys... the late Mark, I assume."

John had said it had been taken care of.

"He was tailing you anyway and set up the shot. They wanted him to believe it was going to be a warning of some kind—not intended to be fatal. He stopped to make sure you were OK, and they apparently decided to silence him."

"Not sure I feel bad about that." I said, although I realize that wasn't really true.

"So at this point you're probably safe," Lang said.

"Yeah, probably," I answered. Not believing a word of it.

Dave and Linda were waiting at the apartment for me, along with Jessie's brother Joe.

"We have to talk you out of this," Joe said.

"Too late," I answered, "the wheels are already in motion. Don't worry guys. I'm not going to be in the crossfire out there. I'm going to be a safe distance away until the cops round them all up."

"Sure, but what happens when they all get out?"

"Hey, they're already trying to kill me."

"Not all of them," Linda pointed out, "not all at once, anyway."

"Sure, but we'll at least know who might have killed Jessie."

"How?" Joe asked.

"Well, I've been discouraging everybody from taking their part in this little drama. The killer had sources at several points in this deal. We'll know who *they* are when we find out who pushed the deal forward in spite of my warning."

"And then by leaning on the killer's accomplices..."

"You got it."

"What if they don't play along?"

"*Then* the killer will probably come after me."

"But..."

"Hey, just keep in mind, he was eventually going to get around to that, anyway."

FORTY—THREE
The Invasion of Canada

"We're not getting anything from the bug," Marchek grumbled.

"I don't get it," Dave answered. "We tested it just fine, and we're well within range. No high voltage… should be working fine."

"Should have used one of *my* bugs." The Fed grumbled.

I shrugged. "We'll just have to keep our eye on the ball then."

We sat in silence for what at least seemed like hours, testing the quality of our mosquito repellent—unable to swat them, for fear of making too much noise.

"I see a light," Dave said.

"Two lights, horizontal," McGowan noted. It's your bikers."

The boat drifted quietly toward the shore. Four men slipped over the side into ankle-deep water. I recognized Pig Iron and Waldo, but was completely surprised to see who was literally holding the bag. My friend Ray-Ray, who had worked over my ribs, was holding an Eastern Airlines flight bag. Apparently providing additional security for this drug transaction.

"Isn't that kid one of Bobby Charlton's gang?" Marchek asked. "Did he switch sides? I have to admit I can't see how the Charlton gang, even under new management, would embrace a bunch of white bikers."

Yeah. What's even worse, if John and the gang were at peace with the bikers, where was my disruption of the deal?

It was just then that two boats, coming from both directions on the river came roaring to the shore with guns blazing. The French contingent, like us, hit the deck, as a couple of bikers opened up in response. Several others jumped out of the boat and began crawling up the shore toward higher ground.

McGowan reached for his radio.

"Not yet," I shouted at him over the gunfire. Wait for our killer to make his move."

"What! They're reliving the D-day invasion out there!"

"Right. So, no real hurry to get your guys shot at. Keep in mind we don't really have any innocent bystanders out here."

"He has a point," Marchek agreed. "You might want to think sort of like a hockey referee during a fight. It's best to wait until one of the sides get tired... or at least until they use up some energy... and ammo."

"There goes one of them." Dave said nonchalantly.

Waldo, our biker philosopher, was wrestling the bag from Ray-Ray who seemed to be badly wounded or dead. He took off running just as the other bikers, who were inching their way up the bank and along the ground to form a Custer-style stand against the invading boats, arrived at the scene. A few shouted, then shots were fired, but they were too busy fighting off the invaders to organize any serious pursuit.

Waldo raced across the clearing toward the far side woods, skirting the Frenchmen who made no effort to stop him and headed toward the road that stood at the corner.

"Now?" McGowan raised his walkie-talkie.

"Sure, hit it."

"All units move into position now! Repeat, now!"

A car came rolling into the clearing and rolled up to meet the running Waldo, while the flashing lights were just visible through the trees in the distance.

"Don't worry," McGowan said. "They're trapped! We've got the road covered."

"What about the trail we used?" I asked.

"Well, I guess we'd just have to stop them, then."

"Who's driving the car?" Marchek asked.

"Lang," I said, recognizing the Chevy rolling along the meadow. "It's my bet he's holding the money for our French revolutionaries."

I swept my binoculars across the far side of the clearing.

"Say, McGowan, you're sure there isn't a trail out through the woods on the other side here?"

"No, it's pretty overgrown. Pretty sure no one can go that way. Blocked all the way to the shore."

"Can they get down the shore?"

"Well, I think you'd break an axle. You'd have to really be desperate…"

"Well, they're desperate enough," I said, pointing in their direction. "Are they covered?"

"We figured the Coast Guard…"

"Might be busy rounding up boats?"

"Shit." He picked up his radio. "This is McGowan," he barked. "Make sure someone from Provincial Police covers the northeast end of the beach… we've got a car heading that way!"

The car stopped for a couple of seconds so Waldo could pile into the back seat.

"We weren't anticipating anyone running that way," he said. We thought they'd never make it…"

The explosion startled us all. I don't think we were knocked down as much by the concussion, as the sensory overload from the bright light in the darkness and loud explosion washed over us.

I fell to my knees as a ball of smoke and fire rose over the wreckage of Michael Lang's car.

"What the hell was that?" Marchek exclaimed.

No one attempted to answer the clearly rhetorical question.

The gunfire, which had gone eerily silent, began again, but weakly. Most of us were still blinded by the light with the blast ringing in our ears.

"Holy shit." Dave muttered.

The sirens and searchlights began to fill the clearing, from both directions. The round-up began.

McGowan shook his head.

"What the hell am I going to charge these people with? There was no drug deal done, any evidence of the coke or the money was blown halfway to the moon and the girl's murderer is smoldering charcoal."

"I don't know. You had three boats full of armed men pull up to the shore. Surely, an invasion of Canada has to violate some sort of law, doesn't it?"

"What about these characters?" he said, indicating the French Canadians

"They'll probably be even easier. They're revolutionaries. Tell them you're charging them with intent to commit treason, and they'll probably demand to be locked up. Any charge for them is going to be just the kind of trumped up case of political oppression they live for."

"Still a hell of a fucking mess."

"Which I probably can't help sorting out. So, since I have a radio show in the morning..."

"Yeah, OK. Get the hell out of here. Thanks for your cooperation." He added with dripping sarcasm.

"Hey, it's what I live for."

Marchek shook his head in amusement.

"You know, Walker, I finally got the report on Matt Royce's military record..."

"Don't tell me... bomb disposal?"

He grinned and nodded. "He went from EOD to the Green Berets. It's worth wondering where he might have been tonight."

"I would suggest we *know* where we he was tonight. We just can't prove it."

FORTY–FOUR
Explanations

*(Announcer)And now Ladies and Gentlemen… Brad
Walker… (Jingle) C K L W… The Motor City.*
  *9 o'clock at the big 8, and I got to say it's not only good to
be free. But it's worth remembering that it's good to be alive.
Here are the Rascals*
Song: *People Gotta be Free.*

"Provincial police are calling it an accident by a group of
men shooting off illegal fireworks." Mac said.
  "Are folks going to buy that?" Allan asked.
  "Well, I suppose it'll create less panic than a running gun
battle between rival drug syndicates."
  "So what really happened?" Allan asked.
  "Why are you asking me," I said. "I wasn't there."
  We were still laughing when the phone rang.
  "Request line…"
  "Hello, Brother Walker."
  "Hello, John."
  "It was a police set-up all along."
  "We were hunting a killer."
  "And you warned me as well. Don't worry, I only used
people I knew to be somewhat expendable. And they had the
good sense to drop their weapons overboard when the law
arrived."
  "Good planning. Listen, a few interested people are joining
us at Sid's Bridge House over here. I figured I could answer any
questions people had about what happened all at the same time."
  "Sounds interesting. Wouldn't miss it."
  "I think," Allan joked, after I invited him, "I'll wait for the
Readers' Digest version."

The man who met me as I left the station could have been
nothing but a lawyer.

"Walker? My name is Thomas Wolarski. I believe you
know my brother Stanley?"

"Don't think so."

"Perhaps under the name Pig Iron."

"*Him* I know."

"He's wounded, and under arrest. I intend to see to it that
you and the police are held responsible for what happened to
him."

"I thought the police didn't get there until afterward, and
nobody there should claim to have seen me at all."

"What! It was your idea! You talked him into it."

"I think you'd find it was his friend Waldo who talked him
into this misadventure... but it's hard to question a dead man.

"I do think, however, I might be able to do one thing for you
guys."

We used the private room at Sid's so Linda could come
without her disguise. If Bob recognized her as the woman in
drag he had met before, he made no indication.

"The deal Jessie came to me after, was a double cross from
the start. The Paladins were bringing the coke, provided by one
of Charlton's associates, across the river, where the transaction
was going to be hijacked by a crew Charlton *hired*. It was
basically a complex version of the usual trade for the Charlton
group. Lang would end up with the coke and Charlton the
money, while the bikers got ripped off.

"But in the confusion, our Jessie, who was acting as a go-
between for the bikers, managed to end up with both the coke
and the cash and, either not knowing the nature of the deal, or
deciding it was an ideal grubstake for her own operation, made a
dash for it, then, after stashing the money and drugs, she made
her way to my place.

"Personally, I think she was playing it straight, but I guess
that Tuesday night, when she stopped here at Sid's in disguise,
she met with Lang who ended up killing her."

"But how did Jessie get involved in the deal in the first
place?" Joe asked.

"She was friends with Bobby Charlton, we found out. He apparently either presented it to her as a favor, or was promising a supply of drugs."

"But she just bought half a kilo of coke," Mac pointed out.

"Yeah, it went to her husband Matt Royce, who had just moved back to the States. He used it both as a source of income and to ease his pain. The idea that Jessie was smuggling into the States sort of took Charlton off the suspect list because as you know, they were moving the flake *into* Windsor. Why would they have a problem with any person trying to bring any back?"

"Speaking of bringing things back," Joe said, "isn't there something we can do for poor Matt Royce... I mean I would have happily done the same thing he did. To have him chased down by the cops..."

"Matt who?" Marchek said. "Haven't you heard this was a fireworks accident? But in case you run across any missing and still wounded soldiers, one of my military sources tells me that a trip to his local VA hospital will leave him with a clean bill of health... In every sense of the word."

"If I see him," said Joe, "I'll mention it."

"I don't think I really got a handle on the case until Charlton was killed. Since he was in Jessie's car it seemed safe to think it was because he thought she might have gotten away with the stash or the cash. Everyone had been pressing me, thinking I had something, but his death suggested a different partnership."

"Why would she partner with him?"

Donovan's question had a bit of an edge to it. He really hated Charlton.

"The more important question was who killed Charlton? The Paladins might have wanted to muscle him out, but starting a shooting match didn't seem like a good choice. It never seemed likely he killed Jessie, so the family wouldn't have done it. But it started to make sense when you added a third partner like Michael Lang."

Lang and his partners were going to screw up the sample deal, then approach the bikers with better 'facilitation' for a reasonable percentage.

The drugs were going to end up in the usual pipeline through Charlton, who was making money at both ends, while the bikers' ripped off money was going back to Lang."

"So the money is still missing?" Donovan asked.

"The money and the drugs. If the cops don't find them in Lang's possession, then they might still be where Jessie hid them.

"After Jessie's death, Charlton must have found the car, then met with his partner, Lang, to split the goodies. When they found the car was empty, Lang either thought he had been double-crossed, or decided Carlton didn't know where the stash was either, and decided to split it only one way. He killed Charlton, then planted his body at the Holiday Inn to divert suspicion."

"Pointing at you," Dave said.

"Possibly, but I think it was, even more importantly, out of sight out of mind. The car had probably been in the Holiday Inn parking lot the whole time."

"Probably," McGowan said, looking at me with wheels turning.

"The truth was, Charlton was my number one suspect until he turned up dead. I was then still leaning toward Mitchell Martin, until Donovan here supplied the critical clue of Lang borrowing his boat only to have the anchor turn up missing. I don't believe in coincidence, so it was pretty obvious she was dumped from the boat.

"One Question was... why didn't Lang replace the anchor and rope? Nobody would have ever remembered a new anchor as well as they did a missing one.

"The second and toughest question was... why kill Jessie? The only reasons could have been personal or because one of her partners, Lang, we now know, was desperate to get his hands on the money or the drugs, but why? It wasn't a lot of either for ambitious dealers, so why the deadly impatience?

"Anyway, it was only a day or so ago when the thought crossed my mind. What if Lang needed the money because it was unique? What could be special about cash? Then I thought about the idea of known money."

"Known money?" Joe asked.

"Lang's Canadian bosses were telling me he had become a wiz at systems to track their money in a secret cash flow business, increasing their financial efficiency. He used things like ultraviolet marking, as well as serial numbers to keep a handle on his organization's money.

"I have to assume our genius must have outsmarted himself by either using his organization's money, or cash that was tagged by someone else, like the Police, FBI, or RCMP."

"RCMP?" McGowan challenged.

"Just an example. The police also mark, or note the bills they use in things like drug investigations or kidnappings. What if the buy money was marked? That packet of money would be a big red finger pointing right back at the source of the buy money—Charlton and Jessie's silent partner—Michael Lang."

"How do you know he didn't get the money back when he killed Bobby Charlton?" Linda asked.

"He was willing to loan money to our Frenchmen for the second drug deal. If he had his first packet, he would have made Marat come up with the whole sum. It was a dead giveaway when he was willing to use his own funds to secretly bankroll our French Revolutionaries.

"You love to call them that," McGowan chuckled.

"Yeah, it's fun."

"What made you so sure he supplied any money in the first place?" Donovan challenged."

"He might not have, but where else would the Frenchmen get US money, the bank? I guarantee the bikers didn't want to be paid in Canadian money."

"Any idea what happened to the drugs?" McGowan asked pointedly.

I smiled a bit. "I might have an idea."

"Well?"

"I said I had an idea. When I know for sure I'll let you know. Maybe they're already where no one can get them. Besides, you don't want me to tell you now, do you? You don't want to have to beat all of these other fast operators."

A few chuckled, but most of them looked warily at the cop.

"Just make sure it's one or the other. I'd hate to have to take you off the air."

"Sure, you got it."

"I'll remove one cop from the party at this point." He said, rising. Take care of yourself, Walker."

"You, too."

"I'm off too," Marchek said.

"Looks like the party's breaking up," Linda said.

I nodded.

"I don't know about you guys, but I'm getting a bit hungry," Dave said. "Maybe we should all grab a bite to eat."

"Sure, are there any good burger joints here in town?" Joe asked. "Hell, I'll even buy."

"Not for me," I said. "I had a long night and an early morning. I think I'm off to bed."

"Want some company?" Linda asked, leaning close to me.

"Actually, darlin', I was really thinking about *sleep*, and you know how you are... listen, go with the guys, keep them company. Maybe after a short nap, I'll be more energetic."

"You'd better be."

"You sure you're OK, Brad?" Dave asked.

"Yeah. I know it's a rare thing, but I just want a little rest."

"I'm going back to brief the boss," Donovan said. "Can I drop you off, Walker?"

"Nope, think I'll take the walk, breathe a little fresh air."

"Suit yourself."

As we were reaching the door, Bob stopped me.

"Aye, glad I caught you. There's a wee package for you at the bar, Mr. Walker. I thought the barman had given it to you, so it was out of mind, you see."

"When was this, Bob?"

"Oh, just a bit over a month ago. That wee fellow with the... odd features, if you know what I mean."

He smiled almost involuntarily as he thought about those "odd features".

"Well, I guess I better take it and see what 'he' left me."

The box seemed neither large nor heavy as I strolled down the street, but this was the sort of day that a little worry seemed like no worry at all.

When I got to the apartment, I carefully placed the box on the coffee table and went to the kitchen for a beer. I was just getting comfortable when the bell rang.

"Come on in," I said. "I was expecting you."

FORTY–FIVE
Behind the Curtain

"You were expecting *me*?" Donovan was a bit surprised.

"There were a couple of other possibilities," I said, "but I knew it never ended at Michael Lang."

His eyes narrowed, then he seemed to relax a bit.

"So you think…"

"Oh, I *know* now."

"Go on," he eventually said.

"You couldn't take a chance that that money was traceable. After all, you had always known Lang was the Canadian syndicate's expert on money security, in fact, I'll bet you've even adopted some of his ideas. Using marked money would have been his perfect defense against your double-cross.

"That's how you two got started, right? Comparing notes on running your respective syndicates? You knew your guys had made a point of staying out of the drug trade, so the last thing you could risk was somebody finding out you were involved."

He nodded slowly, then drew his gun.

"I guess I'll take that package." He said.

"Help yourself." I gestured.

I sat nonchalantly on the couch. He held the gun steadily while he unwrapped a box of sliced newspaper.

"OK, wise guy, where's the money?"

I shrugged. "Not here. I only set up that little package deal to remind you that the money was still out there. Bait for the trap."

Just like me. A big ol' piece of cheese.

He cocked his head to the side like a dog. Then turned and headed for the door.

"So you don't know where the money is, then?"

"Of course I know where the money is."

He chuckled. "You're just bluffing."

"You can't assume that. The point is, you already screwed up when you assumed Jessie had the money when you killed her."

He looked astonished, but I knew it was because he didn't realize how close to the truth I was.

"I killed her?"

"Sure, she died on your boat. She's how you 'lost' your anchor."

"That was Lang."

"Lang was unlikely to have been on a boat, because, according to the Mounties, he can't swim. He nearly drowned as a child and was deathly afraid of water; so he was equally unlikely to have killed Jessie."

"What motive did I have to kill her... a few thousand bucks? I could have easily covered for that sort of loose change."

"But it wasn't the money was it? You arranged the meeting just to intimidate her into giving back the money, but when you two recognized each other, you knew the only way to silence her was to kill her."

"Recognize her..."

"She had told us that she had never been over on this side of the border, so it took a while before it occurred to me she had been seeing you."

"Ha, prove it."

I shrugged. "We know you used to cross over quite a bit as well. By car... then more recently, by boat. It makes sense that you might have met her. Jessie probably wasted no time (she never seemed to anyway) and then you continued meeting in secret on the Canadian side because I don't think your wife would necessary approve of Jessie.

"What I don't get is how you could set up a deal with Jessie and expect her to not know you were involved."

"Are you out of your mind? If I had known that bitch was involved I would have never had anything to do with it. She has been fucking with my sanity ever since I met her. She was a great lay, but, like you said, my wife wouldn't have approved. So she starts following me around, showing up places. Not actually threatening anything, just managing to always keep me wondering where she was going to show up again."

He smiled. "Guess I just admitted something, didn't I? Well, anyway, Lang comes to me with this girl brokering a deal for those bikers, just keeping me up to date, right? So, we got this idea, I mean they were all just sheep to be sheared, you know?"

I nodded as if I understood.

"We needed men, so I talked to some people in Charlton's organization, and they agreed to lend a hand."

"Mark was your pipeline into Charlton's group right? That's why you needed that second boat last night. You had no idea that Charlton's group would show up the second time."

"Yeah, I got a little help from Mitch Martin this time."

"How did you end up killing her?"

He paused for a second.

"Lang said Charlton's girl had the money, so I told him to bring her to the boat. We were just going to sweat her a little. I assumed Charlton's girl was, you know, black, but instead it was *her*! She started out by asking about my wife, and it went straight to hell from there."

"That was what really gave you away, you know. Charlton's murder and the location of his body was clearly personal, and you are the only one whose eyes roll into the back of your head every time his name gets mentioned."

"Killing *him* was a lot easier. I hated that three fingered little spook. He ruined everything."

"Especially Jessie, right? That's why you dumped him in her car. A symbolic burial, as I think you suggested, born in jealousy."

"I don't remember the whole thing, but I do remember gripping her by the neck while she kept lying to me about not having the money."

"She wasn't lying."

"She was always lying."

"She didn't have the money when you killed her. It was already in someone else's hand."

"Yours? Maybe she gave it to you after all ..."

"Nope."

"Perhaps," he said brandishing the gun, "I'll just search the place."

"Suit yourself, I said, but I don't think you actually have any time for that."

"Why not?"

"Because your future is pretty limited."

"So you say." He leveled the gun at me again.

"I think you're not going to be able to do that. You're not exactly the cold-blooded killer. The murders you committed were based on passion, jealousy, greed. No good motive here. Besides, you don't know who else is listening."

"What?"

I reached over to the small transistor radio.

"This is the small transmitter my friend Dave put together."

He smirked. "That was blown to hell with Lang and Wally."

I shook my head "That was why we couldn't listen in last night... I gave Danton the wrong radio. They looked almost identical. When I discovered my mistake last night, I thought of another good use for the thing."

(In truth, I didn't discover it at all. I planned the whole thing.)

He smiled broadly. "So you want me to believe the cops are listening?"

"Now why would I waste this story on the cops? They're busy with clean up and wrap-up. I put you on the air to the two syndicates, Charlton's people and the French Revolutionaries." I smiled my own smile. "Oh, yeah, and the Paladins. You know what's best about this? No trials, no appeals."

His smile faded, then returned, slowly.

"You expect me to just *buy* this?"

"Suit yourself."

He hesitated, then re-aimed.

"Of course you won't necessarily be around to find out if your bluff is successful."

"Oh, I don't know. I think my friend Spiros might have something to say about that."

Donovan laughed. "That's the oldest trick in the book."

"It's only a trick..." I said.

"...when there's no one there." Spiros answered from the kitchen doorway.

Donovan's eyes grew wild for a second as he tried to think of impossible ways to shoot me, turn and fire before the gunman got him. Or turn and fire, then shoot me, or maybe just shoot me, but he indulged that only for a second before his breathing went back to normal, and he slowly lowered his pistol. He looked over his shoulder.

"I guess there's no point in having my gun drawn at this point. Do I get to keep it?"

I looked at Spiros, who shrugged.

"Probably need it later," he said, sardonically.

I nodded.

He placed the gun on the table, and took a seat.

"So we're waiting for the cavalry?"

"Oh, I'm not obliged to keep you here. I don't want blood on my carpet. I just had a few questions, which you answered. I did wonder one other thing though?"

"How can I deny a gracious host?" his voice dripped sarcasm.

"I guess I can understand how Jessie tended to torment people in some ways, and the money, and your hatred of Charlton, but why would you kill her, knowing how her family was going to react?"

"Family… that's the whole damn problem with the Mob. It's always the fucking family. I worked my ass off in the organization for 15 years, practically ran the fucking thing and when the old man kicked off who was the whole thing going to go to?—Joey, the taxi driver, or that little nympho?—hell, he'd leave the thing to that bedbug crazy daughter of his if he could get a coherent sentence out of her.

"And the crazy thing is the others would go along because it's always family with those damn dagos. So I was raising go-to-hell money for the fucking family. I was going to make a load and hit the islands or something.—Retire.

"But now, thanks to you and that bitch, I can look forward to a different kind of retirement."

He reached casually for his pistol. Then a wry smile crossed his face.

"I ought to stay and fuck up your carpet. Take care of yourself, Walker."

"Good luck," I lied.

He walked quietly out the door.

"So who gets him?" I asked.

Spiros shrugged.

"I got ten on his own Mob," I said

"I'm betting Royce," Spiros said.

"Jessie's husband?"

"He got Lang didn't he?"

"He didn't have any help with that, did he?"

He smiled very slowly. "Like Mike Lang said, I get bored sometimes."

I chuckled a bit while I nodded.

"So now you're giving Donovan a head start?" I asked.

He shrugged again. *Talkative fellow.* I raised my hand in farewell.

"Thanks for covering my ass, man."

Spiros kind of smiled, "No charge."

He gave me a vague salute and headed out.

"Good hunting," I said.

Linda was the first to return to the apartment, and was still wrapped around me when the others arrived.

"How did you come across Jessie and Donovan?" Joe asked.

"Well she was coming over... he was coming over. I suspected they knew each other, I think, because of something your mom said about devils who worked for your father. Somehow, I took that to mean your mother might have known about him."

"My mother?"

I shrugged. "I know. She never seemed to get anything, but you know how Jessie liked to tell intimate details of her life to shock people... why not your Mom?"

Joe's eyes narrowed, but he nodded slowly.

"Donovan was a perfect relationship for Jessie, secret, complicated, with her having several ways to make him miserable. Close enough to be practically family, but carried out sort of anonymously."

"So Donovan killed her to keep her quiet." Joe said.

"That's part of it, but I also suspect that there was some jealousy."

"His family rant."

"Yeah, she also had a fling with Charlton, who Donovan completely despised. Which compounded his rage. It certainly was more of a crime of passion than a cold-blooded murder, but the only place that would matter would be in court and there's no danger of him reaching trial."

"OK," Dave said. "We're really going for food this time. And you're coming for sure."

"Actually, guys," Linda said, "Brad has important duties here."

"I do?"

"Sure, you have to pay off on that pool game you lost."

"I lost? Since when?"

"I just ruled that."

"What if I say you're wrong. I never lost."

"Then you must have won." she said.

"I'm ruling it a draw." I announced.

"OK, how would that work?"

"We both have to pay off."

"Now you're talking."

FORTY–SIX
The Silent River

We were lying in bed, Linda curled against my right side.

"Brandy said you kissed her," she teased.

"Actually, she kissed me."

"She's only sixteen!"

"Yeah, but she's been keeping pretty fast company. You do know she's been shadowing you and Jessie?"

"What?"

"Don't look so shocked. You have to remember our little pool party. What do you think those kids were doing out there, the backstroke? About the only thing she lacks is experience."

"You didn't…"

"Nah. I get plenty of action from the varsity. Why try out the JVs."

She laughed. "Good answer."

She dropped her head back to my chest and in a few minutes began to breathe slowly and softly. I thought she was nodding off.

But then: "It's a shame you weren't telling the truth about knowing where the money is." She said.

I grunted assent but made no comment.

"Well? Wouldn't you want to lay your hands on that money?"

"I wasn't lying." I said. "I know where the money is."

She raised her head off my chest and looked sideways toward me. "What?"

"Well, I know who Jessie gave the money to… or did you just take it?"

She sat bolt upright.

"Are you out of your mind?" She squeaked.

"It never occurred to me that you were involved until I realized that Donovan had killed Jessie because she recognized him. He said he knew there was a girl in the deal, but I believed him when he said he had no idea Jess was involved until it was too late."

"Then I thought about how you two love to change places and switch up,"

I smiled involuntarily. Her eyes widened. "I'm betting, since you two love trading places, it was you who were supposed to be at the exchange when all hell broke loose."

"You're out of your fucking mind. You're suggesting I stole from my best friend?"

"Not exactly—it was, after all, your deal from the beginning wasn't it? The bottom line is that you ended up with the money."

"Me? That's insane."

"No. Jessie told someone she had gotten into this thing helping a friend. I had always assumed she meant her husband or maybe Charlton, but I'm not sure she was ever attached to any man other than physically.

"But you two. You were a team. Share and share alike. She would take the risk for you."

She was sitting up, turning back toward me, mouth half open. I raised onto one elbow.

"You worked the bikers, while Jessie handled Charlton."

"You've lost your mind. Gone paranoid. Why? Why would I do this?"

"The money, of course. Not just this little transaction, but you were setting up a working pipeline and a steady income."

"Oh, please, you've been to my house. Do I look like I'm strapped for cash?"

"No, no, it's your Dad's house."

Her lip turned up, halfway between a sneer and snarl.

"All that money comes to you with a price doesn't it. I mean, that little Kelly job doesn't exactly keep you in your accustomed lifestyle, does it? When college didn't work out, you ended up back where you started. It was frustrating, you had started to think for yourself, do for yourself—then suddenly you were Daddy's little girl again. You were falling back under your parents' influence again. It was all very subtle, but you were losing control.

"This was all about you raising 'go-to-hell' money for *Daddy*, wasn't it?"

She turned an angry red.

"What the fuck do you know about it," she snarled. "Having to show up at Daddy's parties and always act like 'Daddy's perfect little princess' and have to be nice to all those leering old phonies and the catty bitches they married.

"I have to put up with my Mom when we go shopping: 'I don't know dear, don't you think that skirt's just a bit too short, too tight, too flashy'.

"Then there's my fucking little sister. Not only do I have to babysit the little bitch, but now I find out she's been trying to take over my boyfriends."

"So the rebellion began. First Jessie, then, of course, those bikers. After a while it wasn't enough to just have a little secret life, you wanted to make a more permanent break from them. A new life."

"Fuck you. What's wrong with having a plan for the future. I swear, you're just like Daddy—you want me to live my own life, but you want me to live the life you want."

"Your plan needed money anyway," I continued, "so you concocted this deal with the bikers. Lang and Donovan were setting up the bikers for a shakedown but instead of just taking the drugs, you shot for the money as well."

She shrugged. "Well, why not. I figured they wouldn't make a big deal over a few bucks. I was just wrong."

"With Jessie dead, you were going to stay out of the way and hope if anything fell it was going to fall on somebody else."

Namely me, but I at least avoided saying that!

"But then your biker friends began to press you to set up another deal, but you didn't want be on the spot, so you roped me into it with your phony kidnapping."

"Phony!"

"Sure. I don't think I ever bought the bikers in Grosse Pointe deal and then there was your friend Waldo…"

She flinched slightly, thinking about his recent demise. Or perhaps, something else?

"I kept wondering how he found you at the Fiddle that night. It was easy to assume he followed you, but the easier explanation is that you called him. About half an hour or so after I got there our guy strolls in. You even occupied my time with a little pool to make sure we didn't leave."

She said nothing.

"Did you have a plan to swipe the money again this time? Maybe you and Waldo?"

She glared angrily for a moment.

"I suppose next you're going to accuse me of killing Jessie."

"No, Donovan did that."

"It was Jessie's idea to take my place that night. And even if she had the money he probably would have killed her anyway, right?"

"Probably."

"There's nothing I could have done to save her was there?"

"Probably not."

"Then why are you busting my ass? I've got no reason to feel guilty."

"Hey, if you need absolution, find a priest. You asked me about the money. I just answered your question."

"You could have lied," she said, petulantly

"Sure, I could have played along… 'You're right, honey, it's a damned shame nobody's ever gonna find that money.' You might not have set Jessie up for a fall, but you did set me up. I just couldn't let you get away with it."

"Get away… Jesus Christ!"

She levered herself out of bed and turned, naked, to face me.

"Is that what this is about? Suddenly you're my fucking conscience? Well you can go straight to hell, Mr. Jiminy fucking Cricket!"

She turned toward the door, scooping up her dress and shoes in full stride, with surprising grace, then marched out of the room.

"Hey!"

"What!"

"Before you storm out of here, could you at least let me know what this master plan you needed the money for was? What did you want to do? What's it all about, Alfie?"

It was a minute or two before she returned to the doorway, her dress draped over her right arm, shoes swinging hypnotically. She posed subtly.

"You want to know?"

"Well, yeah."

"Really want to know?

"Yeah!"

"Good. Suffer. Burn." She turned and left, thumping down the stairs. After a couple of minutes, I heard the door slam.

But she returned, dressed this time. "You're going to laugh," she said.

I shrugged.

"I'm going to be an actress."

I nodded. "Sure, you've got talent."

"You promised not to laugh! I've wanted to be an actress since I was a little girl on the TV show. I loved it all. The lights and the people and the attention."

"One, I never promised not to laugh. Two, I've seen your recent performances, like 'I'm scared of the bikers', which was pretty good. In fact, your 'I wonder where the money is' was great. I would have bought it if I hadn't known better."

"Fuck you."

"Now there was the virtuoso performance," I said grinning.

"That will never happen again."

She left the doorway, but I didn't hear her on the steps.

"Brad..." A little girl voice.

"Yeah."

"You're going to eventually forgive me, right?"

I had no answer. I understood everything she had done, whether I approved or not. But the bottom line is, we could never quite trust each other the same way. She had used me and she was going to have as much trouble with that as I was.

I got up and walked to the window, looking at the river. Peaceful to watch for the first time in weeks, it seemed.

"Maybe," I finally answered, "but probably not tonight."

"I know. For what it's worth, I love you."

"Love you, too."

The apartment door closed quietly this time.

The Story of Brady Ellis

Photo by Karen Maier

A while back, Writer Jim *Ellis* was having a beer (or three) with his buddy, Radio Host Jim *Brady*, when Brady turned and said, "I'm thinking about writing a book."

OK, Ellis thought, Brady has 40 plus years in the radio biz—easy to figure he had enough material for a memoir. He's a better than average storyteller, so he, just trying to encourage his friend, heard himself say, "Sure, Brady, I've got some free time."

(The part of my head working on my own writing projects was screaming *'Have you Lost Yo' mind!?'*--Ellis)

Then, Brady rolled the grenade into the room. Not a memoir, but murder mysteries based on his days in radio. So the way it works, Brady supplies characters and situations, while the novelist/historian Ellis supplies a little historical detail and does most of the #@&* typing.

It's worked out well. We remain friends and haven't killed each other, *yet*… stay tuned.

Find the authors at their local pub, or www.brady-ellis.com